The Idle *v*: other ta\

Wendell Harris

Part One
Faded World

3 x Me

The first time I saw myself was from a bridge I was standing on near the old campus where it meets the canal. I was on the bridge and at the same time, I could see that I was on the far bank of the canal below me walking away. We wore the same clothes, a padded green duffle coat with a fraying hem, blue jeans and mock Italian loafers. The only difference I could see was the canvas satchel slung over one shoulder. I watched myself pass between some bushes, follow the dirt path round a corner and disappear behind the pool hall. I would have liked to follow myself and learn more but I was already late. I turned back towards the campus and passed through the old buildings till I reached the ringroad, then went over the pedestrian crossing on my way into town.

It was two years later that I was walking along the canal, with my green satchel full of leaflets that I was hoping to distribute. It was early autumn again, with that same feeling of rain and cold on the way. Just before I got to the turning by the pool hall I thought to look back at the bridge, but I was no longer there.

The second time I saw myself I was in the campus library with a borrowed card, trying to find books on the Wilshaw Riots. I went out to the fourth floor foyer to work out how many books I could reasonably fit inside a supermarket carrier bag, lamenting the loss of my satchel on an unrelated train journey to Mablethorpe. At some point, frustrated by the endeavour, I went to look out of the window where I saw myself below, standing on the bridge, watching myself as I walked along the far side of the canal (the old familiar satchel swinging by my side), tightening my coat in anticipation of the cooler weather. I could see that I was tempted to follow myself, but eventually came back across the bridge in this direction, until the angle took me out of view. Slowly and absent mindedly I went back and started stuffing my preferred books into the plastic bag. I knew that one of those people would have luck and the other wouldn't. It all seemed so inconsequential and a bit sad.

After that, I never saw myself again. I wonder if I'm still here.

Blue Crystal

I wouldn't normally have been in the supermarket at that time but I'd been given the morning off unexpectedly. They had the usual stuff on display - aspic, brine - but then I see the special offer: blue crystal. I went over to the hard mineral aisle and there it was, a pyramid stack of boxes, all emblazoned with their gaudy logo. Who could resist? I picked up a box and took it to the checkout, forgetting everything else. When I got home I couldn't wait, ripping the top off the box and pouring the crystals into a bowl. They gleamed and shimmered, making a tinkling noise as they clattered off the porcelain. The sight of them gathered all together in the bowl gave me great satisfaction. I spent the rest of the day filling in the holes I'd made recently in the plasterboard walls of my flat and whistling merrily.

Walking into town the next day I saw the crystals being advertised on a billboard - limited time only. I hurried to the cash machine at the petrol station and withdrew one hundred pounds, then went back to the supermarket, buying twenty boxes. Fortunately, I had enough change left for a taxi, so I was able to transfer them from my shopping trolley to the boot of the cab and get home. I got the boxes out of the boot of the cab and stacked them on the low wall in front of my block of flats, then took them upstairs five at a time. Once they were all inside, I breathed a sigh of relief and moved them on to the kitchen counter. It wasn't good enough. I ended up taking my collection of old sports bags out of the cupboard in the hallway, so that I'd have a place to store them safely. Of course I'd missed my appointment in town, but that could wait. Now I had to find someone who would buy a collection of old sports bags. Feeling pretty good

I fished the phone out of my coat pocket and started ringing around.

I ended up trading the sports bags for more bowls to put the crystals in. Soon I had roughly one hundred bowls all around the flat, and in each one, the crystals lay glittering and twinkling. It never got boring because you could move the bowls around. The one problem I had was that one box had contained green crystals instead of blue and I didn't know what to do with it. In the end I took it back up to the supermarket for a refund but by that time it had disappeared. Typical. They always disappear and you have to wait for another one to pop up somewhere else. That left me with a box of green crystals that nobody wanted. I even tried leaving it outside in the hope that somebody would steal it, but it was still there ten days later. Even the charity shops didn't want it. Three months later a man called round at my flat, saying that he'd heard I had some green crystal to get rid of. I was so relieved. By that time, I'd hidden it away at the back of the cupboard under the kitchen sink, and tried to counter the disturbed feeling it gave me by placing twenty bowls of blue crystal on the coffee table next to the sofa and watching reruns on the television. I went downstairs to let the man in (I'd been talking to him from out of my living room window which faced onto the street). Once inside he seemed amused and dismissive of my amassment of blue crystal. Even scornful. He was a man in his late forties, still with a good head of greying hair and a straggly beard, dressed in a brown suit and trainers, no tie. I fetched the box of green crystals and his clear blue eyes lit up.

"At last," he said.

He grabbed the box out of my hands, a cracked smile splitting open his face like a cut tomato. He stared at me delighted, manic even. "This is it! Thank you! Enjoy your BLUE crystal." He started laughing, really howling with laughter. "Enjoy your BLUE crystal!" I let him stagger his way over to the front door. "Ooh Hoo!" he laughed. "Ooh Hoo!" Eventually he left, leaving me feeling annoyed, angry actually. "Take your stupid crystal" I thought. "GREEN crystal. Idiot!" I slammed the door behind him. That night I couldn't sleep. I kept getting up to rearrange my bowls of crystal, dissatisfied. But the feeling went away after a few days.

Two weeks later my friend Terence was driving me down to Luton. There was a warehouse there on a trading estate, rumour had it, with surplus stock, several crates of blue crystal included. I'd cashed in all my savings in the hope I could get down there before anyone else heard about it. I also had to cancel my shifts, which didn't go down well, but my growing lack of enthusiasm for the job had been noticed anyway. It didn't matter. Terence was only too keen to help. He'd seen the bowls of blue crystal in my flat and understood their importance. If only he'd seen the potential himself he said, but it was too late now, unless he could get a crate off me in lieu of petrol money. Begrudgingly I agreed. When we got there the leaseholder of the warehouse was waiting outside. We shook hands and he undid the padlock, letting the shutters roll upwards. There was various surplus inside, but what caught my eye were the ten metal cages, each holding twenty boxes of crystal. I was overwhelmed, my heart started racing. There was, I think, a strange sheen on my face.

"How did you get all this?" I asked

"Shop in Stockton," the man said. "They only want red crystal down there." I looked the man over. He was short with a trim sandy moustache and a mop of tangled hair, wearing a chequered shirt and grey workpants crumpled around the knees.

"Red crystal" I mumbled. "Good luck with THAT."

I handed over the cash and we started pulling the wheeled cages out, so we could load the boxes into the van. It was a steady half hours work, but invigorating. Each box I lifted seemed to add to a feeling of sublime satisfaction. I could sense Terence's mixed feelings of amusement and envy as he glanced over occasionally, trying to keep up with my brisk pace.

"Never was a man so happy," he said. "Never so happy"

Instead of putting the new crystals in bowls, I used some ornamental planters that I picked up in the gardening section of a hardware store. Each one was full to the brim, glittering shining loveliness. The hue emitted by all the bowls and planters imbued the whole flat. It was like living INSIDE a crystal. That made me think .. I plucked a crystal out of a bowl and looked at it really closely. Inside was a little frozen man. I picked up another, there was a woman inside. I felt that they were all happy. I went over to the sofa and turned on the television. They were advertising green crystals.

The Circular

It was five AM on a frosty morning as I waited for the train at Harsam Newsley. Dark. Over the station wall I could see the roofs of houses and the odd street light. Nobody else was waiting. I walked about a bit hearing my footsteps crunch. At six minutes past the train arrived, three carriages. I got on board and saw there was one other passenger, half asleep, wrapped in a heavy coat, scarf, wool cap, arms folded tight around himself. I took off my gloves, stuffed them in my pocket and sat down, watching the platform slide away as we pulled out of the station.

The train went through the suburbs passing the backs of people's houses. Occasionally I saw the upstairs light in someone's window, the occupant getting ready for work or just restless somehow? More passengers got on in the dark at Octon Regis, Benjamin Farlow and Mersley, and I could see it was starting to snow. Big wet flakes against the window. By the time I arrived at Burlington Minor it was already several inches deep. I got off the train and crunched through the snow, putting my gloves back on and fastening my coat. I made my way over to the lockers and found number 13, took the key from my coat pocket and opened it up. The parcel was inside, wrapped in brown paper. I took it out and slipped it into my other coat pocket, being careful to keep it separate from the pocket where I would keep my key and gloves, then crossed the station bridge over to the adjacent platform. It seemed to be getting lighter although the snow was still falling, drifting lazily around me. While crossing the bridge I saw several streetlights blink themselves out, though the town was still quiet. There were two other people on the platform and I looked at the clock. Ten minutes.

By the time the sun had risen properly we were traversing fields on the way to Morton Gormley. The snow made everything very bright. The hems of my trousers were still wet. But the sun melted the snow and when we pulled into Morton, water was dripping from the station roof. By the time we got to Fluxbridge Parlour it was nearly Spring.

I left the train and was glad to see that the cafe was open. I went inside and ordered the breakfast. For the first time that morning I heard people talk, low murmurs from the customers around me. It still being cool, there was condensation on the windows. A damp, merry air. I wandered around Fluxbridge enjoying the fresh breeze. I could smell the leaves waiting to unfurl on the trees. I delivered my parcel and obtained the receipt, which I was able to cash at a local bank. The cash went into my inside pocket, separate from my key and gloves. It was much warmer when we got to the next town and I was able to fold up my coat and put it on the seat beside me. The train was livelier now, full of gossip and business talk, and outside everything was green and there were leaves on the trees. We passed through a number of small stations and it was Summer by the time we reached Nookworth Point. Carrying my coat over my shoulder I went out into Nookworth. It was a historic town with lots of small shops on the outskirts. I found the one I was looking for, a specialty store with a red painted entrance and leaded windows. Inside I bought the recommended item, this time a wonderfully painted tin box. I asked for a plastic bag into which I placed the box, with my coat laid carefully over the top. Then, feeling I'd proceeded correctly, found a nearby pub in which to have lunch. There was a good crowd, more locals than visitors and I spent more time in there than I should have, needing to move briskly in order to make the five o'clock train to Tarbow Southpoint. By that time Summer was over and I could feel the leaves ready to leave the trees. Rains started to shower the windows all the way to Tarbow and I looked sadly at the backs of industrial estates, stock yards, sports pitches, all the usual detritus you see through the window of a train. People were on their way home from work, more tired than talkative. I relieved myself in the Tarbow station toilets, admiring some of the more obscene graffiti, then went down the platform stairs into the scruffy street. There was a red tiled pub on the corner, some boarded up shops, and luckily a newsagents nestled amongst them. I bought some tape and brown paper and wrapped up my tin box. Outside it was raining again, so I took my coat out of the bag, placed the parcel in the pocket and discarded the bag in a nearby dustbin, before returning to the station.

It was getting dark and cold again by the time I arrived back at Burlington although the rain had cleared. Surely now it was almost Winter. Autumn had left puddles, wet leaves and sodden clumps of litter in the streets. We pulled into the station and I went over to the lockers. I unlocked number 13 again and placed my parcel inside. Then I returned to the railway platform. It was almost empty, just a young couple sat shivering on a bench, ready for a night out somewhere. She wore a bright green dress, and he wore a salmon pink shirt, having taken off his jacket to wrap round his paramour and keep her warm. They laughed at something and it echoed across the empty train tracks. But that was none of my business. I waited for the last train that would take me back home. No doubt, there would be frost in the morning.

Imps

Like most people now, I needed something to do that wasn't productive and pointless, so I started taking photographs. Specifically, photographs of places. There was a website that linked your photographs to survey coordinates on a map, so people could see what was there without actually going. The photographs didn't have to be especially scenic and many people, like me, seemed happy to itemize the mundane aspects of existence. My own preferences were for takeaways, municipal substations and storage facilities, in that order. Not just taking the pictures of course, but listing those taken by other people. Wednesday's jaunt however was different, for it took me out into the countryside. A new idea had taken hold of me, and I intended to catalogue the minutiae of farming life, starting with cattle feeders and watering troughs and their various substitutes (such as old baths or industrial bulk containers), then moving on to sheds and the like. I was also interested in the plastic wrapped hay bale, that had all but led to the extinction of the traditional haystack. I had chosen a very fine August day, and in some instances I had to avoid the temptation to actually TAKE scenic photographs. But no, I had a purpose to fulfill.

The next day I was editing the pictures on my laptop when I noticed something strange. I was certain, in the background of one of the pictures, in a stand of trees behind a grazing area, there was a concealed figure. In fact, I would not have noticed him at all were it not for his white mask. A strange shock went through my body, and I felt a hesitation in taking the natural next step, more of an aversion, to zoom in on the picture. When I did it, I did it very carefully. The figure had no reason to be there, and of course, I had noticed no such thing on the day itself. His mask was white, the eyes round, black and hollow, red circles were painted on the cheeks and a fixed yellow smile was painted below the nose. It gave me a dreadful chill. Was there such a horrible personage lurking around the countryside and I'd chanced upon him, without noticing? It was ghastly. Should I tell someone? I didn't know. I checked through the other photographs. There was nothing there of course.

It took me a long time to get to sleep, and when I did, I dozed for maybe an hour, waking up with a bothered feeling around half past two in the morning. Without really thinking I went into the living room and turned on the laptop, then started opening up folders, searching through all my old pictures. Twenty minutes later there it was. A picture of an electrical substation next to a nursing home. Looking through a window of the nursing home was the masked figure. How hadn't I noticed it before? I had a terrible feeling of dread. I felt suddenly that the whole flat was floating alone in the early morning dark. I made myself look out of the windows. There was no one down there out in the street, no one in the carpark. The other windows were virtually adjacent to a raised playground and I had to raise the blinds to look out. I hesitated, then did it quickly. There was no one out there either. Just a splash of light from the mosque's security lamp. I felt foolish, but still couldn't stand to sit there with the blinds open. I lowered them back down and stood in the kitchen with a coffee until dawn. When it was light enough I went to the website and checked the same picture online. The figure was still there in the window, but different, as though it had moved. I checked. It had moved. Slightly backwards and to the left. head tilted as though talking to someone.

It took all my efforts to persuade my friend Bernard that I wasn't playing some joke on him with photo editing software. He was even skeptical when I asked him to look through the rest of the photos, although something in my demeanor must have eventually impressed him.

"Here it is. Here it is." he said, turning to check my reaction. That must have impressed him most of all because I simply swallowed up my lip and pulled a knee up to my chest, grasping it tightly. "You don't want to look?"

I shook my head, then said, "Show me."

He turned round the laptop so it faced me. It was the Fortune Chicken restaurant in Luxby with the bookmakers next door. In the shadows of the bookmakers you could just see two masked men sat at one of the checking tables looking out. I had taken the picture a year ago. I shook my head again.

"Check the website," said Bernard.

"I didn't post that one."

"Well, it's unlikely they could both sit there like that without inviting comment from the proprietor."

Bernard turned the laptop round again and zoomed. There were the same painted red cheeks and yellow smile on each, just noticeable in the shadow.

"Someone playing a joke on you?"

"Who? Who even knew I was going to the countryside, never mind got there before me? Who plans jokes over a year?"

"An elaborate prank that's all it can be. Think. Who could it be. Jonesy?"

"Saved the image off the website? Reuploaded after making alterations? That's very elaborate. And what about the one I didn't post?"

"Still I'll check. Tell people 'ha ha' but its really messed you up."

It was the only hope I could feel.

"If you would."

I could hardly say I didn't want to spend the night on my own, so I went out instead, moving around the pubs until I ran into an old workmate. Even though I'd quit all that nonsense a while ago I made a big deal about him and his friends coming round for a smoke after closing time. Mind you, I could only do that once.

After that of course nothing happened, but I was unable to bring myself to go out and take more pictures. Bernard never did find anyone willing to own up, though that didn't stop him needling me.

"Any more ghosts?" he'd ask.

I found it more difficult as the year drew on and days began to get shorter. I found myself going out more to avoid sitting around while it was dark outside. I was always looking around, even at work. One day I thought I saw one under the trees on the far embankment while I was bringing cages into the loading bay. I propped the freezer door open before I went back in, scared of being trapped inside somehow. Two nights later I came back home drunk and feeling the need to make a show of bravery I pulled up the blind on the window facing the playground. There were three of them sitting on top of the slide looking towards me, white masks and yellow smiles gleaming in the dark. One by one they stood up and floated in through the window.

The Hound

The monitoring centre was in reality a portable cabin propped up on concrete blocks on the edge of a tarmac lot, surrounded by a fence of vertical steel bars and barbed wire. Just before midnight I parked up outside and went over to the gate, then took the phone from the pocket of my black security jacket and keyed in Jon's number.

"You here?" he said.

"I'm here."

I heard the locking mechanism of the gate unclunk and let myself in. The light above the door of the cabin came on. I could see our own camera next to it, covering most of the lot, and the electric cables that stretched from the roof of the cabin to the top of a nearby telecommunication pole. Jon turned round from the monitors as I entered.

"Anything?" I asked.

"Nothing."

I sat down on the chair next to him. Jon wheeled his chair away and picked up his book and thermos. We watched the screens for half an hour each, then swapped over, to maintain concentration levels. The other then, ostensibly, handled the phone.

"Good book?" I asked.

"It's alright. Biography of Emelyn Hughes."

He was pouring coffee. We monitored six locations, each covered by 3-6 cameras, 24 monitors in total. Hardly anything ever happened. We switched over and I got out my phone to play Zip Zap.

"I thought games were for kids," said Jon.

"I thought biographies were for boring old tossers."

"Touche."

"Anything?"

"Drunk in the foyer."

"He gonna fall over?"

"Nah."

"Why are you bothering me then?"

"How about you turn the stupid bleeping down."

I turned it down.

The monotony was broken during my third half hour.

"Jon. Come look at this."

It was the Fenay trading estate, exterior. A man outside dressed in a dog suit, the kind you get for fancy dress, comical.

"What? What an idiot!"

"How did he get on to the estate?"

"Drunk. Climbed the fence. Stag party?"

"Idiot"

The figure had stopped in front of the camera monitoring the outside of the industrial units. He stopped and looked right up into it, then did a little dance. Sort of a bend your knees, wiggle hips, piston your arms kind of dance.

"Fucking comedian." said Jon

"Call it in. Don't want the prat to hurt himself. Cover our arses."

I watched the monitor as the funny man waved at the camera then ran out of view.

"You don't think he knows we're watching?"

"Fucking dipstick doesn't even know what he's doing."

The phone rang back just as Jon was packing up to leave.

"Centre 377."

"You the jokers rang about a guy dressed as a dog?" His tone told me they hadn't found him.

"We called that in, yes."

Jon was hanging round to hear the rest of it of course. I made a 'this could be awkward' look with my eyes.

"There's no fucking guy dressed like a dog round here. You on a wind up?"

"No. Want to see the footage?"

"There better be fucking footage or I'm putting my boot up your arse. I had to drive in from Bexley."

"I'll send you the footage Clive, keep your knickers on."

I hung up as he mumbled. Jon and I looked at each other, then started laughing.

"Well, some good came out of it."

"Fucking Clive. Wind back the footage, let's watch him looking around again."

"No, I'm going. Watch it with Tariq if you want. See if you can cheer the bugger up."

My mobile started ringing. I picked it up and looked at our camera monitor.

"Tariq. I'll buzz you out at the same time."

Jon nods, and goes out the door chuckling to himself.

The second time we saw the man in the dog suit was much stranger. This time he was in the foyer of the Franklin building. It was strange because we only monitored the six locations, and no one outside the firm had a reason to know which ones. It couldn't be a coincidence.

"Jon jon jon" I said, pointing at the monitor.

He looked up. "Son of a bitch." Immediately he wheeled over.

"It's the same guy?"

He was in the foyer looking up at the camera. He did the dance again.

"Same guy."

"But wh.." He wheeled over to the phone then hesitated. "Clive. Getting his own back."

"He got hold of the same dogsuit?"

"Online. Sure, why not?"

"Nah. It'd be a disciplinary. Anyway, he's on duty isn't he?"

I looked back at the monitor. The man was still looking. Then he waved and went over to the stairwell.

"He's going upstairs."

Jon was on the phone. "Clive. We've got the comedian. Dogsuit."

Silence, then what sounded like a rush of expressive language from Clive. I was watching the first floor landing. Dogman reached the landing, then went through the doors into the first floor corridor, waving to the camera as he went.

"First floor" I shouted over, then added in a lower tone. "What if he's a psycho? Fuck."

"Clive, we're serious. First floor. We think the guys a nutcase."

Clive and Ahmed pull up outside the Franklin building in the firm van. It was a town centre residential, that had security fitted to monitor the occasional bit of lairiness that overflowed from two bars down the street.

"If the joker IS here." says Clive. "I'm going to clock him one as soon as we reach a blind spot."

"You think he's a nutter?" asks Ahmed.

"Don't know. But we've got lone females on the first floor. You got the heavy torch?"

"And steelies, yeah."

"We see him, we stay back and radio the police."

They enter the foyer and Ahmed phones Jon's mobile.

"Any movement on the first floor?"

"None. Still up there as far as we can tell."

"Okay, keep your phone on."

They reach the first floor and Clive shines his torch through the corridor doors before pushing them open.

"Security! Everyone alright up here?"

No answer, so they go looking up and down the corridor.

"You hear anyone awake?" asks Ahmed. "Maybe we can knock on some doors."

"And say what?"

"We don't mention the dog thing obviously. Just if they heard someone moving around."

"Fine," Clive sighs. "Hello. Anyone awake? Building security.."

"And nothing?" asked Jon.

"Hardly any bugger up. A couple watching late night tv, so they say. Didn't notice a peep. Show me that fucking footage again."

We play the footage back over the monitors - dogman on the first floor landing, gives the camera a wave.

"And the fire exit. Camera on the stairwell?"

"Yes, but nothing."

"The other floors."

"Nothing."

"Guys guys guys!" says Ahmed.

There were five of us in there by now, Clive and Jon both past their shift. Ahmed points over to the monitors. Dogman is back in the foyer of the building. He walks back and forth with a jaunty sort of sideways motion, arms out at his side like chicken wings.

"That little fucker thinks he's funny." said Clive.

"Let's not waste our time," I say. "Leave it to the police."

"You know how funny they're going to find us, if we do that?"

"You want to chase the guy around?"

Clive sighed. "Okay, call it in," he says.

The next sighting was two weeks later. The police had found nothing of course, and couldn't do anything. Ahmed and Clive had been posted to the foyer of the Franklin building, alternate nights, which pissed them off. We could watch them on the monitors though, and radio through emergency calls:

"Ahmed!?"

"What?"

"You look bored."

"Yeah, fuck off."

This third time he appeared on the third floor of the Hawthorne building, the office suite where they had a safe for cash payments - not massive amounts but still. He was sitting at someone's desk, wheeling the chair from one side to another, holding his hands out to his shoulders as if to say - 'I'm here. Why are you waiting?"

"That is fucking it," said Jon, getting to his feet and gathering his jacket.

"No, no Jon. We don't do that."

"The Hawthorne's three minutes away. I'll be on him before he's expecting it."

"Not on your own."

"Watch the monitor. Tell me if he moves," and he was out the door.

I swore under my breath and watched him cross the lot towards the gate. I buzzed him out and rang his phone.

"Leave the phone on in your car." Outside I could hear his Saab start up and drive off. I watched the monitor. A minute passed. Dogman held out his arm to look at an imaginary watch, then looked up to the camera and held out his hands again with a shrug.

"Jon," I said, "I think he knows you're coming."

"What do you mean?"

"He's acting like he's waiting for you. Jon. You're not forty any more mate. Lets call it in."

"Don't worry. I used to kick whole firms of hoolies out of the Apollo. I can handle this nonce.. anyway, I'm here."

I looked at the monitors and saw his car pull up outside the Hawthorne. He got out and strode over to the entrance, still with the phone held to his ear. Switching my attention to the third floor I saw dogman's head perk up as though he'd heard something. He looked at the camera again then raised up his fists to each side of his head and shook them in a silent hooray. Then he got up and moved offscreen. I swerved the camera, tracking across the office in time to see him leave the suite in the direction of the stairs.

"Jon," I said. "He's coming to you."

"Right," said Jon, voice tight. Military. "Radio silence."

I watched him stride across the foyer, check the stairs and slip the phone into his pocket in exchange for a pair of knuckledusters. Old habits. I lost sight as he decided to take the ground floor stairs. Everyone was out of camera view. I waited. Waited. There was nothing until the dog's head sprung into view of the foyer camera, filling the screen. He must have been standing on a chair. I wheeled my own chair back from the monitors in alarm. A pair of costumed hands reached up, detached the fake head and lifted it up. Underneath it was Jon, face mangled and covered with blood. I started to scream.

No. 39

 I got on the bus at Talbot Street. Not many passengers that time of day: an old lady with a pink coat and matching hat and two shopping bags, and a young man in his twenties with shaven blonde hair and a tattoo sliding down his neck into the collar of his jacket. We drove up to the bungalows where the old lady got off, giving me a sympathetic look and shaking her head as she did so. What did that mean? I turned around to observe her through the window as the bus pulled away. She was standing there and looking around her at things only she could see. I watched her take something out of one of her shopping bags - but then the bus went round a bend and she moved out of sight. Later we were passing through a rag tag district - garages, warehouses, student flats and two girls got on. Just in time because it was starting to rain. They sat down next to each other and one of them plugged a set of earphones into her phone, putting one plug into her right ear, while her friend put the other in her left ear. There was the faint tinny sound of music. It might have been irritating, but fortunately my stop was next. I got off. Everything seemed normal.

Edith picked up her shopping bags and hobbled onto the bus. It was empty, apart from an unkempt young man who looked blearily out of the window and rubbed his eyes. She sat down glad to rest her legs. The bus pulled away from the minimart and set off down the high street. She was pleased to see that the birds were out in number today. Great flocks of parrots lined the rooftops, while some grebes and cormorants were gathered around the fountain in the precinct. There were rooks perched on the lamp posts like sentinels and the grouse were hobbling down the thoroughfare.

There were no more passengers until the man got on at Talbot Street, seemingly oblivious to the pelicans gathered on the wall behind him. Never mind. Edith got off at the bungalows, where a whole host of thrushes, tits and wrens flew down from the rooftops where they'd been congregating and gathered around her feet, or rested on the brim of her hat and on her shoulders. She sighed ironically and took a packet of seed from one of her shopping bags.

"Here you are birdies," she chuckled and started scattering the packet's contents, the bus disappearing around the corner in the distance.

Daniel sat on a marshmallow in the bus station. The bus pulled in, a big sponge cake with sugar glazed windows and liquorice wheels. He paid the driver with shortbread and the bus set off through the town centre, with its jelly shops and pudding houses. An old lady got on outside the stack of sugar lumps that made up the minimart, both her shopping bags bristling with butterscotch and aniseed. After that, a shabby looking middle aged man got on at Talbot Street, sherbet pouring out of his eyes. The old lady disembarked by the bungalows - lumps of toffee amidst lollipop trees, and Daniel watched as the candy mice scurried around the corner to greet her. After that, he fell asleep for a little while. It had been a long night, dancing with the caramel ladies at the Yum Yum club. When he woke up, treacle rain was beginning to fall from the sky.

It was starting to rain when the bus arrived. Charlotte and Wendy hopped on board, avoiding the screechers as they flew past. There were two men on the bus, their clockwork faces continually interlocking into a series of different patterns. The bus driver pulled his lever and the cogs started to churn, gripping the chainlink road and dragging the vehicle forward, as the people in the streets around them were sucked through the vacuum tubes that passed between the buildings. Charlotte turned the dial on the side of her head, and the cable connecting her face to Wendys began to pulse. One of the men got off the bus. He plugged his face into a nearby terminal and they watched his body fold up into a series of neat boxes.

Containers

I drove onto the Fenshaw trading estate and manoeuvered my truck until it was parked outside units 6-12. 1-5 had brown corrugated shutters with the large yellow numbers painted on. 6-12 had red shutters with white numbers. I could see that 1-5 were already in overspill, some of the protoplasma having forced itself through the seals onto the roof, where it sat gently pulsating. A container was waiting for me, as was Taff.

"Looks like you've got problems," I said.

He rolled his eyes. "Gordon messed up the order, didn't he? Now we have a surplus."

"Well, we best get this one shifted then."

"Where's it going, Shibden?"

"Toxteth. They're having an issue with some lichen."

"Everyone's got problems by the sound of it."

"Never was a truer word said Taff."

He got on the forklift and started to raise the container. I heard the lifting mechanism squeal as it took the strain and Taff tried to keep balance.

"It's flubbing about in there!" he shouted.

"Steady boyo!" I looked on, worried. That damn stuff was getting more temperamental all the time. To our mutual relief, Taff managed to load the container.

"About time you invested in a hoist," I said.

"Tell them that" said Taff, pointing towards the office building. "I had enough of a time getting them to buy me some oozeproofs."

I set off towards Toxteth. The drive was without incident. The big red warning decal on the back of the container meant that most people tended to give you a wide berth. Occasionally, through the back of the cab, I could hear the plasma flubbing about in there - flub, flub, flub, flub. It could be unsettling. Approaching Toxteth I could see they had issues. Lichen was sprouting out of various drainage outlets and was starting to spore. I pulled up outside the depot, then had to get out of the truck to buzz the intercom next to the gate.

"Plasma delivery," I said. The gate whirred and moved aside as I got back into the vehicle and drove into the yard. Nazeem was waiting for me.

"Where do you want it?" I asked.

He directed me towards the fluid traps underneath a storage tank, which were clogged with lichen. Netting had been put all around to catch the spores. I reversed so the back end of the container faced the traps, then got out of the cab.

"How did it escape?" I asked Nazeem.

He scowled underneath his wool cap. "Same way it always does. Waits til there's a vent open then spores. It's getting smarter if you ask me."

I looked at the lichen, a blue green feathery mass with its sprouting nemapods.

"And now it's in the drainage," I said.

"Yes."

"Fuck. We best get on with it." I collected the ratchet from the floor of the cab and went round to the back of the trailer. Naz watched as I cranked the lock then pulled back the bolt, swinging the door open. We stood back as the protoplasma tumbled out of the back of the truck, pulsed and dilated then slid rapidly over the yard towards the lichen. It started to devour it, absorbing the fungal mass, which screeched horribly, a high pitched strangled sound that echoed around the yard. Then the plasma let itself ooze between the grates of the trap and went into the system. The screeching carried on all afternoon.

"They're going to have to stop using so much lichen, it carries on like this," I observed.

"But then what do we do with all the plasma?" replied Naz.

I took time to consider the matter. "True. Especially if Fenshaw keep overordering."

"Again?" He shook his head. "What do they do with the surplus, when it gets restless?"

"Their problem. Was out on the fucking roof when I left."

"You're kidding."

We both shook our heads. The screeching was getting fainter, moving further away.

"You want a fresh crate?"

I checked the docket, nodded. "Blue container. Harvested lichen, 100 kilos of, if you please." I stuffed it back in my jacket pocket as Nazeem went over to the forklift.

"Any chance of a coffee?" I shouted.

He gestured towards the portacabin that served as a canteen. "Second shelf. Don't use Malcolm's cup."

I headed back to Armley with my new load, getting caught up in traffic on the outskirts of town, the school run snarling up vehicles all along westbound. I took the time to consume my sandwiches and surveyed the giant metal cages that lined the nearby horizon. I could hear the chirping of the aphids from here. I got out my earplugs. The noise was veritably intolerable as you neared the complex itself. The traffic cleared enough for me to turn into a backstreet I knew would bring me near to the back of the complex if I could clear a tight junction next to the refinery. I swung the truck around, perfectly, and feeling pleased with myself, made the delivery just five minutes behind schedule. Warren was waiting for me.

He pushed himself away from the wall he'd been leaning against and motioned me over towards the silos. The earplugs we were both wearing meant there wouldn't be much conversation. I parked up and he clambered on board a forklift, unloading the container and reversing back into the silo. I left the cab and followed him inside. Once the door closed, we were able to talk.

"Busy?" I asked.

He nodded, and truth be told he looked tired. "Non stop. Ever since a bunch of them got loose and flew into town. Flew right through the windows of a tenth storey office. Fucking pandemonium. We're still paying out in compensation apparently."

"They ate some people?"

"Just three. It's not our fault. They get bored of lichen and who can blame them?"

Two young lads were already rolling the lichen out of the container and putting it onto trolleys, to take up to the feeding bays.

"No, but it's the only thing that works, so they tell us."

I left the silo and climbed back into my cab. It wasn't a bad job really. The two lads who'd unloaded the container would spend the rest of their shift collecting the protoplasma that spilled out of the aphids carapaces, once the insects had finished feeding. They had a lot of work to do. Fenshaw had just ordered twenty tons.

A sketch, a poem

I settled down at the desk by the open bay window that overlooked the park, a fresh breeze fluttering the net curtains and bringing the smell of the leaves indoors. Under such conditions I felt, a man could write one of the fifty immortal poems. As it was, I wrote a story about a butterfly trapped in a lift. It was haunting, enigmatic, but not yet immortal. I sighed, screwed it up and threw it in the wastebin. Then I took my jotter and my biro and went out for a stroll. I sat for a while on a park bench and felt the sunlight. Flowers were moving around in the breeze. I watched the people. Perhaps their faces would suggest a great story. But all they suggested was resignation. I started to write anyway. A lady sat beside me and asked me what I was writing.

"A story" I said. "Would you like to hear it?"

"Yes, of course, " she said.

Of course implied that people always wanted to hear my stories. Nothing could be further from the truth. I was lucky if they wanted to hear me talk at all. Something had happened recently. They felt at liberty to cut me off and talk over me halfway through any sentence I uttered. Maybe I'd just turned into an incomprehensible idiot? So I felt less flattered and more as though I'd come into contact with the miraculous.

"Ah well .. it's a story about a man and a woman"

"Is there any other kind?"

"They meet in the snow at a railway station. He's struck by how vivid her dark eyes and red cheeks seem against the snow, and she's struck by.. whatever women are struck by.. his brooding nature?"

"Maybe the way his face suggests crocuses waiting to bloom under the snowfall."

"Damn, that's good. Now I have to rewrite."

"What do they say to each other?"

"He asks her if she expects the train to arrive. She says she does and that it will travel through the snow for six months, but the carriages are warm and opulent, and the company and food are always good and people drink good wine and tell fascinating stories through the night, and sometimes there is love and when you're in your berth and the train is travelling, rattling through the dark with the snow outside, it feels like you're the only two people in the world."

"That's the story?"

"Oh no. Halfway through the journey they stop at a station. It's still piled high with snow. A man gets on, an old man but lively, with obviously many stories to tell. That night he regales them with the tale of the fox, of the time he went hunting as a young man, and he chased a white fox through the melting snow and it led him to a lake."

"Twas not a lady bathing in the lake, twas there?"

"No, because the lake was still frozen. But there was a lady under the ice. He sat there two weeks waiting for the ice to melt and the fox brought him scraps of food to eat. The lady became his wife but he never told anyone how he found her, just said she was an orphaned bit of skirt."

"But he tells the story now?"

"While he's drunk to strangers."

"And what happens when they arrive at their destination?"

"Well. I was thinking of having it as an Arabian Nights type thing, where they hear a different story each night. But when they arrive the snow has melted, and it's a busy town and they have to go about their business and quickly they forget all the stories and even what attracted them to each other in the first place."

"Aww, that's sad."

"Well, happiness writes in white you know."

"How many stories do you need?"

"Six times thirty is one hundred and eighty. The arabian nights had a thousand, I think, but that was a collaborative effort."

"I know a good story."

"I'd love to hear it."

"It's about a woman who used to come to the park every day and sketch the people, and one day she saw a man in a bay window, in a house opposite the park, trying to write something. She thought he might be interesting so she made a sketch of the two of them sitting on a bench talking."

"And this is it?"

"Yes."

Bald Tom

Bald Tom drove to work, listening to conscious hip hop on his car stereo. He worked at the Social Improvement Centre, teaching the idiots there how to make art. He had lots of hacks to make art seem easy. Look how easy I make it seem, he liked to say, even I can do it, haha. If you follow the hacks your art will turn out looking like mine and that means that it's good. Beryl's works were terrible both in subject matter and execution. No matter how hard she tried to follow the hacks they turned out the same - obese men with big hanging dicks and blood slavering from their mouths. They spoiled the atmosphere of the Centre, which otherwise was decorated with Tom's abstracts, cleverly referencing a range of artists and combining their styles into a pleasing mish mash, or ornamental handicrafts from the Wednesday Club. Somehow, Beryl's work made Tom angry. I think it was the repetitive nature of it, just fat men with their ludicrous members and slack mouths. He was still angry as he drove home. Trying to improve Beryl was taking attention away from the rest of the group. Gordon, for example, had successfully managed to copy Tom's style and was almost as good. He was so preoccupied that he didn't notice the fat naked man trying to cross the road in front of him, and when he did, he was so shocked by the size of his phallus that he failed to apply the brake. The man smacked into his bonnet, went right over and smashed through the windscreen. His head hung over the dashboard, drooling blood into his eyes. The conscious music kept playing over the stereo. The man, as it turned out, was simply a local schizophrenic who'd skipped his meds. That wasn't enough to prevent Tom being convicted of death by dangerous driving. Suspended sentence, but it meant he was unable to keep his job at the

Improvement Centre. Eventually, after his divorce, he found work clearing litter from the railway embankments. Ten years later he attended the opening of Beryl's first major exhibition at the Tate Modern. He still hated it and failed to understand.

The Walled Garden

Gwendoline tried playing croquet on the lawn, but it was terribly dull and bothersome on her own, and Lucy, her ragdoll, was no help at all. If only her brothers weren't away at boarding school, or Henry the gardener wasn't in Brighton with the missus. Even nursey didn't have time to waste on 'daft games', and her mother was suffering from one of her turns. Which left Gwendoline with no one to play with but Lucy and Tibbles, the Irish terrier.

"Well you are no use at all Lucy. Can't even hold a mallet silly doll. And Tibbles just runs around scaring all the hoops."

Tibbles woofed in agreement and went back to running around with no good purpose whatsoever.

"Oh, this is so silly. I'm going to the garden to get your ball Tibbles, then at the very least you'll have something to chase."

She skipped across the allotments, waving around poor Lucy in the most haphazard manner, and went into the walled garden. It had tall walls of red brick. There was the arch through which Gwendoline had passed, and over the top of the left hand wall - just - she could see the roof of the big house. There were stables on the other side of the garden, and to the right, the peachery, its trees in full blossom. In the wall connecting the garden to the peachery was a green door that was always locked, presumably to stop people scrumping the peaches. "As if I would," thought Gwendoline. There was a sundial in the middle of the garden, flowering plants all around the edges, and a bench along the left hand wall for sitting and thinking. It smelt of jasmine and lavender.

Gwendoline eventually found the ball, which had rolled under a clump of marigolds, when she heard a knock on the door.

"That's peculiar," she thought.

Tibbles stopped his excited scampering and pricked up his ears. It was peculiar because the peachery was also surrounded by walls and the only way in was through the garden and as we have said: the door was locked, although it could be unfastened from the other side. There was silence, then a knock on the door again.

"Hello?" said Gwendoline, not because she wanted to but because no other course of action seemed quite proper. If only Henry was around. The door unfastened and pushed open a little and poking through it came a soft white snout. It waved around and snuffled, tasting the air, then a mouselike creature, the same height as Gwendoline and walking upright on its hind legs, came through the door. Mouselike, although its proboscis was longer and more flexible than a mouses, and it only had one big eye resting on top of its head and it walked on blue penguin like flippers. Apart from that it was like a mouse. But with no tail.

"Oh," said Gwendoline. "Who might you be?"

"I'm Tony," it said. "More to the point, who might you be?"

"My name is Gwendoline," she replied, "and this is my family's garden if you please." It was difficult to resist making the point.

"Your family garden is it? Well, well, what a strange place to put it." The eye on top of Tony's head began to swivel as he looked around.

"Strange. Why strange? And if you don't mind me asking, how did you get inside the peachery? Did you burrow in?"

"Burrow?! Certainly not," Tony huffed. "I was simply walking through the park, and then these strange trees turned up, and then I was here. A peculiar anomaly, but I suspect this explains matters." He waddled over to the sundial.

"Is that the amolony?" asked Gwendoline, looking bemused.

"Anomaly girl. And not quite the thing itself, though maybe the cause. Yes, yes. Whoever did this was quite the smarty pants. Tell me, do you have any clever ancestors your family told tales about?"

Gwendoline blushed. She really never paid as much attention as she should when people told her such things. It always made papa rather cross.

"I -I don't really know," she confessed.

"Ah." The eye squinted. "Well I'd find out if I were you. It might prove to your benefit."

"Can you show me," Gwendoline asked, "how you got into the garden?"

"Show you? Hmm, well. We should see if it works both ways I suppose. Yes, come." He turned around and went back through the door.

Gwendoline hesitated. She was very sure papa, not to mention nursey, would not approve at all. But she did ask the question after all, and now it would be rude not to go. "Look after Lucy, Tibbles," she shouted, and all of a rush, ran through the door into the peachery. She could see Tony not far ahead, walking between the trees, and yes, there did indeed seem to be more of them than before, and there were no walls except for the one behind her.

"This is a strange basket of apples and no mistake," she thought. Then, scared to be left behind, ran after Tony, looking all around as she did so. The peach trees stretched endlessly out into the distance in every direction, but then there were different trees, ones with great feathery blue leaves and puffballs on the end of their stalks, and then when Tony stopped, they were in another place altogether.

"You see," said Tony.

"Yes," muttered Gwendoline as she blinked her eyes, "an alomoney."

Besides the trees, the park had yellow paths that wound around large pink craters, which were filled with tinted gloopy liquids, and when she peered inside, peculiar fish like undulating sacs of jelly with fins and eyeballs on stalks. Then there were the birds, furry things that flew by means of propeller. The sun was pale green, and three moons span rapidly around it.

"What a topsy turvy place you come from!" she exclaimed. The day had turned out not to be so dull after all.

"Topsy turvy indeed," he harrumphed. "You might be the one who's lopsided girl, think about that." Indeed, Gwendoline's appearance was starting to attract attention, and several mousey creatures, who had been enjoying a day in the park, were now gathered around and speaking to Tony in a series of staccato whistles and pops.

"They're asking how on Gnaffid you got here. We haven't had one of you here see for six hundred years."

"And that is how you learned to speak English I suppose."

Tony giggled. "Oh no. I completely lack the vocal apparatus to speak your language. What I can do is send out a mental transmission that allows you to translate my speech for yourself."

"Tramsnissions and wotomalys. Even when you speak english it is double dutch." Gwendoline was quite pleased with that witticism, which seemed very grown up, "Why don't you just say magic?"

"Magic, yes. That is a good way to explain it actually. Now if we walk this way a little, these ladies and gentlemen want to ask you some questions.

Gwendoline thought that sounded a little dull, like lessons, but as a guest, supposed it was expected of her. And it was a small price to pay, for the chance to keep exploring. So she agreed and altogether, they set off for the city, with its buildings like pastel coloured termite mounds. When she woke up, she was back in the walled garden, lying on the grass. She blinked and looked up at the sky. "I must have fallen asleep," she thought, "but what a peculiar dream." She sat up sharply and looked towards the door. It was shut as though nothing had happened. And of course, it hadn't.

Tibbles was sat on the neatly clipped grass, staring curiously at Lucy, who lay face down on the path next to a flowerbed.

"Well speak up Tibbles, did you see what happened or was it a dream?" But Tibbles of course said nothing, not even a bark. Seeing that she was awake, he just picked up the ball that was next to him, trotted over and dropped it back down. She picked it up, stood and threw it out the arch back towards the allotments, then went over to the peachery wall and tried the door. It was locked of course.

Several times that year, Gwendoline dared herself to go back into the garden, always taking Tibbles with her, but nothing ever happened. Once, she even asked Henry if she could go into the peachery, on the pretext of pressing some blossom for her scrapbook. But the peachery was just as it always was, twenty or so trees surrounded by four walls. So in the end, she came to the conclusion that it WAS all a dream, and over the years it faded into the vaguest sort of memory, one not remembered at all except as a notion. There was one time when she ventured into her father's study to ask him who built the garden. He looked up from his papers in surprise. It was quite unlike Gwendoline to take even a halfway serious interest in such things. So even though he was tired and preoccupied, he took the time to stop and think about it.

"That will have been your very distant ancestor .. yes that was the third Lord Massey if I remember .. late 1700s .. come, I'll show you." He led Gwendoline from the study into the library, all the way up to a portrait on the south wall. The man in the painting was handsome, raffish. "Here he is .. bit of an odd duck by all accounts .. stellar reputation at Oxford. Took the grand tour, made a diversion to Mesopotamia, then went exploring out in the colonies. Made some pretty good finds too .. you can see them in the British Museum. Settled back down here at some point and built the garden. Come this way" They went round one of the bookshelves to the next bay, where there was another portrait. "His wife Charlotte .. looks rather like you Gwennie, now that I think about it, how you might look when you're older. There'll be an account of the old boys travels somewhere hereabouts, and plans for the grounds too. But you'll have to find those for yourself gal, I have business needs taking care of." He ruffled her hair, pleased with the idea that she might find a sensible use for her time.

And the funny thing was, Gwendoline did turn into a serious young lady, and the walled garden one of her favourite places to read. She felt an attraction to it that she couldn't always account for. It was an autumn, in her fifteenth year, when it was really getting too cold to continue reading outside, and the peaches were starting to drop from the trees, that she heard once again a knock at the door.

She looked up hastily, and the memory of that first knock, all that time ago, sprang back into her mind as though it had only happened last week. She felt the grip on her book tighten, and her heart quickened in her chest. The instant was frozen, and the spring of yesterday merged with the autumn of the present so it was hard to tell them apart.

The knock came a second time, and she remembered to breathe.

"Yes" she heard herself say, and the voice was strange and quavering.

The door unbolted and a man came through, the man from the painting of course. Older than in the picture, and strangely attired, but still with that raffish quality. He grinned.

"It is! Young Gwen. But look at you..."

She looked at his odd clothes .. smooth and silky with bulky pockets and clunky boots. "And you are .. Lord Massey?" she ventured.

He beamed again. "Yes. I can see that you did your research. But that needs some explanation I suppose. Did you ever figure out the sundial?"

She shook her head, obscurely ashamed.

"Well of course you didn't, what am I thinking? Not yet! But it was the Gnaffids you met the first time, the mousey things?"

"Yes, Mr Tony, they were taking me up to the city ..."

"And then you don't remember very much."

"That's right! That's why I thought it was a dream."

"Now that is a concern. You'll have to excuse me Gwen, but there's something I need to check." He sat down next to her and turned her nose anticlockwise, until there was a whirring sound and a panel opened in the back of her neck. When he looked inside, he could see that some spongey cubes had been attached to her vertebrae. He whistled. "The little buggers. They must have had you apart like a frog .. but it seems like they put you back together properly, apart from a few additions." She heard a snipping noise, then he was holding the cubes in his hand. There was a whirring again and the panel closed. He turned her nose the right way back.

"Oh my," she said. looking at the cubes "what are those?"

"Something like a radio, except they transmit on a very long wavelength. They must have been recording everything you've seen since you got back. Your mousey friends way of doing research. Luckily, out in the open, they should dissolve in our atmosphere." He flung them over his shoulder, into the flowerbed behind them.

"The absolute cheek!"

"It is something of a liberty, I have to admit. So, the question has to be asked .. do you want to go back through the door?"

She rubbed the back of her neck. "Well, you understand if I have reservations."

"Absolutely."

"And I have a question of my own," and her expression now turned shrewd. "If I don't go through the door, how do I end up in the painting?"

He roared with laughter and slapped his knee. "That's right! Oh my girl. Smart right from the outset weren't you? A delight .. an absolute delight."

"So I should stay, make all of this impossible."

"Your choice, gal." Mr Massey studied his fingernails, looked up again and grinned.

Gwen rolled her eyes, and whistled. Tibbles came through the gate into the garden, trotting more slowly now, older. She picked him up, put him on her lap and scratched his head.

"Tibbles come too though, isn't that right Mr .."

"No, Walter, please."

"Walter .. you'll have me back won't you, in time for tea?"

Walter grinned. "They won't even know you're gone," he said.

Spores

By the time I woke up, the fungus had consumed the left side of my face. It was one of those puffball type fungi so I was all lumpy. It had spread from my lower cheekbone, over my eye and temple and almost to the crown of my head. I was able to talk, and see out of one eye. In retrospect, perhaps I should have called in the council, instead of trying to deal with the mushroom myself, but it had seemed so straightforward. I'd prised it off the fence outside with a spade and was taking it to the dustbin when -'pop' - it exploded into a cloud of spores and some of them flew into my face. Irritated, I went into the kitchen where Jen was making coffee.

"Well, that's annoying," I said.

She turned around, "What's annoying?"

"This on the side of my face."

"Oh yes, that does look bad. Have you seen the doctor?"

"I'll make an appointment."

"I'm working outside today, do you think it's going to rain?"

I looked out of the window. Jen's faith in my ability as a cloud reader was touching. "It might," I said.

"I'll take a jacket. Don't forget the doctor."

"I won't."

I couldn't get a doctor's appointment until the next day, so I went to work. I walked through the kitchen and clocked in.

"Morning," said Shabaz, the duty manager, "everything alright?"

"Well yes," I said, "apart from this thing."

"What thing?"

"The fungus," I said "On the side of my face."

"Oh yes," he said "that's not going to be a problem with your shift is it?"

"I'll manage."

"Of course you will. Just remember to rotate the dairy. Some milk was over date yesterday."

So I started work. The fungus didn't really seem remarkable to anyone, despite the fact that it was spreading down to my shoulder. As usual, I was probably making too much of a big deal about things. My jacket was becoming an awkward fit though, lumpy bumpy, riding up on one side. I made a mental note to ask for a larger size.

The next day the fungus had expanded so that I had one 20cm in diameter protruding from my forehead and it was all across my lower back. I went down to the surgery in time for my appointment with Doctor Miller. I sat myself down.

"So, what seems to be the problem?" he said.

I pointed to the mushroom emerging from my forehead.

"Oh yes, that does look sore." He prodded it. "Uncomfortable?"

I shrugged.

"Well, take some aspirin, it will probably go away on its own. These things tend to, don't they?"

So, that was that. Reassured, I went back to work. The big puffball made it awkward to wear my cap, so I came out of the freezer with a numb head. Also, the cold punctuated the fungi so I could feel how its mycelium had embedded itself in the muscle and cartilage of my face. I went home tired.

"How was work?" asked Jen.

"Same-o. How about you?"

"The kids were running around like little animals today, I don't know what's got into them. And Eric took his clothes off and ran around the corridors again."

"Too much sugar."

We ate our chili con carne. It was difficult to swallow.

"I went to the doctors by the way."

"Oh, what about?"

I pointed to the puffball.

"Oh yes, what did he say?"

"Take an aspirin."

"Ah, that's alright then."

I wondered.

The next day the fungus was everywhere. I lay in bed until I
heard Jen leave for work, then got up and stumbled to the
mirror. I was one big puffball. I tried to get my clothes on but
they wouldn't fit. I mumbled something to myself and could
hardly hear it. I stumbled into the living room and tried to
pick up the phone. I couldn't, it was useless. I collapsed on
the sofa and lay there exhausted. I could feel the puffballs
throbbing and knew something was going to happen. At
some point in the afternoon I exploded. The spores floated
around the room for a while, then settled in the carpet and
walls.

Jen got back from work after another exacting day. Eric had
managed to get into the staffroom and urinate over the
walls. Now there was a report to write. She put the leftover
chili in a pan to heat up, went into the living room and turned
on the tv, then looked around. Something was missing, but
she couldn't work out what it was.

postscript

I was walking down the street when I noticed something
unusual. There was a block of flats across the road, and on
the second floor, one of the flats had enormous puffball
mushrooms extruding from the windows. The walls pushed
outwards and bulged, so the whole flat must have been
consumed by fungus. As I watched, one of the mushrooms
'popped' and sent a vast dark cloud of spores across the
neighbourhood. Some of them brushed my face as they blew
past. "Really," I thought, " the council needs to do something
about this." I walked down to the main road, where a man

was watching me from the other side. The rivers of violet ran down his face.

Part Two

The Subliminal Vector

My House Has Many Mansions

I picked up the bag from the floor of my office and went down to the basement. I felt the bag squirm as I unlocked the door. Once inside I turned up the furnace, unlocked the hatch and threw the bag inside. Then I went back to the office. Miss Edison was waiting for me.

"One of my cats is missing," she said. "I was wondering if I could put up some posters."

"Of course you can," I said. "Which one is it?"

"Oswald, the tabby. Have you seen him?"

"No, I'm afraid not. You can use my printer though, if you need to make posters."

"That's okay. I have one for work. I just need help putting them up ... and if you could ask the other residents .."

"Of course. Give me some posters, I'll put some in the communal areas, and I've got some tape you can use - if you want to stick some up outside. How long has he been missing?"

"Three days now. I don't know how he got out."

"Well, he'll probably turn up."

"Probably yes." She didn't seem certain.

I rolled up the posters and took them with me as I went to replace a striplight on the fourth floor. It was a routine task and didn't take long, so afterwards I pinned one of the posters to the corridor's noticeboard. That held me up just long enough to be spotted by Mr. Dixon as he came out of the lift.

"Ah Bill," he halted and said, as though the sight of me had just recalled the problem to his brain. "That reminds me .. the tiles in my bathroom .."

"On my list, Mr Dixon. Talbot have given it the okay."

"Ah, good." He came over. "Is that one of Sarah's?"

"Yes, haven't seen it have you?"

He shook his head. "Oh no, I'd have said something. Keeps them all in her flat doesn't she?"

"Lets them run in the corridor sometimes, but only when she's about."

"Guess one made a break for it ...'escape from crazy cat lady!'"

I smiled. "Probably got lost, being a housecat and everything."

"Yes, that's the problem isn't it? Trying to keep cats in a flat. They're wanderers really."

He had a holdall slung across his back. A mewling came from inside it that we both tried to ignore. I watched as he went down the corridor and entered his apartment, then collected my stepladder and dead striplight and took them back down to the office.

Once inside his apartment, Mr Dixon puts the holdall on a chair and goes into the kitchen. He takes the bottle of pills and dirty saucer from out of his coat pocket, puts the pills on the counter and washes the saucer. From the kitchen window he can see down into the street below. Across the road, Miss Dixon is taping one of her posters to the side of a bus shelter. He smiles.

Miss Dixon has just finished taping the poster to the side of the bus shelter when she feels something brush her leg. She looks down and sees Oswald, smiling up at her in the way cats do. She bends down to pick him up.

"Oswald you silly cat! Do you realise the fuss you've caused?" She rubs her face against its fur, then turns him round to look at him. "Never do that again. Mummy was very upset, you hear me?" Then she kisses him, picks up the plastic bag with the posters and tape, and carries him back inside.

I arrived at work the next day and Miss Dixon was waiting in the lobby.

"I just wanted to give you your tape back Bill," she said. "Oswald turned up, you see. Wasting all our time he was."

"Glad to hear it, Miss Dixon." I took back the tape. "We were worried he'd got lost."

"No, he was just causing mischief. I'm sorry for wasting your time."

"There's plenty of people do that Miss Dixon, and you're not one of them. No.72 for example."

"Oh yes, I can imagine." She rolled her eyes and chuckled. "Well, you have a good day."

I took the tape back into my office, picked up a bag and a spade and went out into the refuse area. It was collection day and the bins needed pulling out. There was one of those things again. Luckily it was groggy from the rat poison I'd put down, so I battered it with the spade, stuffed it in the bag and took it down to the furnace. I didn't see the point in wasting time on another phone call.

Norris leaves the apartment block and walks down to the bus shelter. He has two library books to return, then a date, hopefully, with the girl from the coffee shop. So he'll end up taking something pretentious out, instead of the book he wanted to read. Hey, why not both, he thinks to himself. He checks the timetable then notices the poster taped to the side of the shelter. I've seen that cat before, he thinks, somewhere in the building .. He fumbles a jotter and a biro out of his pocket, makes some quick, scrawled notes, just as the bus comes round the corner. Damn it. He puts them back, flags the bus hurriedly and searches for change. By the time he has sat down, the idea that seemed so urgent has started to recede. He takes out his notes and tries looking at them - 'Dixon goes out at night'. No, it didn't make sense.

Birds

The owls watched me as I walked into the cafe. There were three of them inside, sat on stools, eating at a ledge that ran alongside the window. They watched me as I walked past the window and entered the cafe, then their heads swivelled to follow me as I headed towards the counter. It was hard to work out what their problem was but I knew you had to be careful. They were big owls, probably a foot taller than me, and there were some other birds sat at the tables, geese and ducks mainly. They talked in quacks, as you might imagine. I ordered a latte and the green bean salad, then found a table to myself. It was a cheap and cheery formica table, just like in the old days. The main difference was the birds. I'd just woken up one morning and they were there. It was hard to get your head around. The worst thing was, trying to tell people about it. As far as they were concerned there'd always been birds. "Yes, but didn't they used to be smaller and fly," I'd say, and they'd look at me as though I was mad, sometimes even walk away. Yes, you had to be careful.

There was no incident in the cafe, so I went on down to the market. You can guess what it was like there - crows, sparrows, finches. Altogether a rowdier sort of avian. There was a raucousness to the atmosphere. I tried not to nudge anyone as I passed through the crowd, wary of getting a peck. I ran into Colin at one of the bric a brac stalls, looking at a porcelain dining set. The plates were decorated with charming scenes: swans on a boating lake, rowing their boats and tossing morsels of food to the hungry people who swam alongside the vessels.

"Busy today," I ventured.

"Always on Tuesdays. Looking for anything in particular?"

"New chisel."

"There's a kestrel down there doing tools. I bought some electrical tape off him last week."

We chatted a bit and I enquired about his wife, who had just come out of hospital. She was stable but scheduled to go back in for follow up surgery. It was a partridge performing the operation which could mean trouble - they tended to be mischievous. Colin bought the plates and we moved on, coming to a halt beside the multi storey car park. A finch drove past on a moped.

"Listen," said Colin. "I need someone to take care of some deliveries for me .. while all this is going on. What do you say?"

"Well sure," I said, "if I can. I've got work though."

"We'll fit it in around your shifts. There's only two drop offs and I can do cash in hand."

"Okay, what's the cargo?"

"Six crates of dormice for the fancy restaurant downtown: Hooters, and some assorted grubs and seed for the grocery near Leyland."

"Pick up?"

"I've got a unit near the viaduct, I'll send you the keys."

After making the deliveries I was left with a sackcart that I needed to return to the unit. I parked up outside, undid the shutter and let it shuffle upwards, taking the sackcart from the back of my van and putting it back in its corner, and then for some reason deciding to look around. There was not much left to look at. An old armoire, six Goodyear tyres and a cardboard box filled with Penguin classics. I leafed through them: To Kill a Mockingbird, Swallows and Amazons, One Flew Over the Cuckoo's Nest. It was strange, but the similes employed by the authors suggested that birds were indeed smallish creatures that flew through the air, and had little capacity for dealing with any kind of technological society. I went over to the armoire, and on the same impulse, opened the drawers. Inside one of them I found a framed photograph - a Victorian family feeding ducks at the park. It confirmed all my latent memories. But where had Colin obtained these items? And why did he keep their existence locked away?

Faces

They took my face in part payment and started using it to advertise some products, which was flattering I guess. They sent me a replacement of course, but it was rather bland and non-descript, and I have to admit, I found the lack of attention it brought to me unsettling. Then I had to get used to walking down the street, seeing myself on billboards advertising perfume, or on the television promoting skincare products. It was tolerable, up to the moment I saw someone wearing my face at a local restaurant. She was happy, flirtatious, obviously on some kind of date. I considered going over, but to say what? Instead I went home and rang the company. When I eventually got through and lodged my complaint, they drew my attention to the small print of the contract - 'the creditor retains rights to the aforementioned article, including the option of making the rights available to third party individuals.' Well, I was in no position to afford a lawyer obviously .. it didn't seem like there was anything I could do.

More and more people started wearing my face as the year went on. It was very popular, and people even started making their own modifications to it. At the same time it seemed like I was becoming more and more invisible. I had trouble getting served in shops. People refused to acknowledge me. Then one day I go into work and Janice on reception asks: "Yes, can I help you?"

"It's me Kirsty," I say.

"Kirsty who?"

"I work here."

She looks skeptical. "Really, since when?"

"For six years, I'm in Substitutions and Mergers."

"Let me check." She taps her computer. "Yes, we used to have a Kirsty in subs, but she was dismissed for non attendance, her position has already been filled."

"Well that's outrageous, can I talk to Helen please?" It was strange, her attention was already starting to wander, as though I wasn't there.

"I'm sorry, what were we talking about?" she said.

It was useless. I left. Something made me hang around outside until lunchbreak. I saw the subs team leave the building together and head for the deli. There was only one new member of staff among them. She had my face.

Being without a job turned out to be not too big a problem. My lack of noticeability made shoplifting absurdly easy. I got used to walking into shops and pretty much taking anything I wanted. Both my neighbours and landlord became convinced that I'd moved out, and in the end, it was easier to move into a flat in a cheaper part of town than keep on trying to prove otherwise. The landlord there lived out of town and all I had to do was keep on top of the direct debit. I made money by selling stuff that I'd stolen from shops online. In fact, my entire existence had become anonymous, electronic and I moved through the real world like a ghost. Whenever I did venture out, I estimated that around a sixth of the people were wearing my face, or some variation thereof. I saw myself with larger eyes, wider lips, different skin tones, bone structure .. it was eerie.

Eventually the term of the contract ended, and it was time to get my face back, but by this point it seemed redundant. It had long passed into the public domain, and for me to wear it again would make no difference. Who would believe I was the original? Instead I walked into the offices of the credit agency. No one noticed I was there. I walked into the office of a CEO and closed the door behind me. I chloroformed her and started to unscrew her face. Now we were getting somewhere.

A-Z

The A-Z discount store on Gatling St was run by a Kurdish man called Mr. Benduni. Sometimes, on religious holidays, he wore a fez, but today was not one of those. I had gone inside looking for a pair of needle nosed pliers, but it seemed likely, that as per usual, I would be leaving with more items than originally intended. It truly seemed that everything in the world, excluding groceries, clothing and high end electronics, could be bought there and at such knockdown prices!*

*excluding also vehicles, livestock, and all the other things you're thinking of to try and be a smartass.

In order to accommodate this, strange things had been done to the laws of physics, so that the aisles inside were able to turn in on themselves and run on ad infinitum. It was extremely easy to get lost, and so there were regular notices reminding you of the 'daedalus' method of returning to the till where Mr Benduni was waiting patiently and reassuringly - keep on making right turns.

So on this visit I had already added some batteries, rawlplugs and one of those pocket guidebooks (A Field Guide to European Birds by Colin Winterbroom) to my intended singular purchase.

Then somehow I crosscut an aisle and ended up in Trinkets. The first few items were none too unusual - rabbit's feet for luck, monkey's paws for curses - when I came across the real deal: splinters of the Ark, three for ten pounds!! Well, mama didn't raise no fools. I added those to the stack of items I was trying to keep clasped together with my spare hand.

When I made it back to Mr Benduni's counter, it was hotter, more humid than before, and the light outside, such as you could see behind the mass of promotional items stacked before the window, was bright and hard.

"Be needing suntan lotion if this keeps up," I observed.

"Oh we have that as well sir, factors 5 to 75, very good deals," said Benduni, not missing a trick. I was about to answer when I was distracted by the cawing outside. Tremendously loud, the kind of cawing you'd get if it was made by a lizard rather than a bird.

"I might also recommend this sir," he added, bringing a spray canister labelled 'Repellent' up from behind the counter and placing it before me. I wasn't sure I had enough change left.

I emerged from the A-Z into an early Devonian landscape. This was astounding obviously, and when I turned back towards the shop in search of some sort of rationalisation it had disappeared. As though by magic. Which I suspect it was. So there I was surrounded by fern trees, with lots of trilobites scurrying along the nearby shoreline. Whenever they spotted something edible, like a massive millipede, they would cluster over like a great scab until it was eaten, and when a pterodactyl soared overhead they would separate and flee the way cockroaches do when you flick on a light. But the real predators were in the sea. You could see the waters part into great foamy crests as some segment of them broke the surface, a leathery mass and they were gone. Five hundred yards along the stony shore was the Ark where it lay beached. It looked as though it had been there for centuries. Interesting. I was getting some idea of how Mr. Benduni went about his business.

Gnaffid Revisited

Gwen drove up from London for her father's funeral. Afterwards there was the awkward business of dealing with the family estate. A changing world had made the estate more and more expensive to maintain, and though her father had done his best in his waning years, the war and the death of her eldest brother had broken him in all ways. Now there was the unpleasant task of deciding what to sell off. It was a sombre, rainy day and she stared through the window at the bare trees that hung in the distance, at the edge of the grounds. Her gaze turned towards the old walled garden and she felt a twinge of something, before her attention was taken by Edmund calling from the library. She left the drawing room and walked down a corridor to see what he had discovered, some very saleable books no doubt. Instead, he was looking at the portrait of Lady Massey that hung on the south wall.

"This painting is the spit of you Gwennie, did you ever notice?"

She reflected. Didn't someone else say something like that once?

"Is it?" she said aloud.

"Yes, and the dog, didn't you have a terrier like that. Tombles or something?"

"There is no dog in that picture." That she remembered distinctly.

"Of course there is, look."

She went over and indeed there was, and more over, the lady in the portrait did look like her - Regency fashion not withstanding - and the dog exactly like poor old Tibbles, who'd gone missing that day and couldn't be found. It was the darnedest thing. She thought it over and thought it over but couldn't come up with an answer. The painting must have got misremembered somehow, that's all.

Except, as the day went on, she began to recall the conversation with her father all that time ago, and his showing her the picture, and being certain there was no dog, and his mentioning Lord Massey's journals, and it being in connection with a plan of the grounds for some reason. But she never had got round to reading the journal, still going through her foolish phase. So, amidst all the organising, she scoured the library until she found them, an 18th century manuscript bound in red leather. Before starting to read, she looked up at the painting of Lord Massey III, that hung adjacent to that of his wife. He seemed amused.

"But it's raining Gwen," said Edmund, "and we still have an awful lot to do. What's so important about the garden?"

"Just something I need to see," Gwen replied, and they arrived at the garden she hadn't thought about for many years. She had a recollection of reading here, long endless summers in between the rains, and a strange story she'd made up about the place as a child .. the one that had caused her to talk to her father .. but now the garden was abandoned. The flowerbeds were bedraggled and overgrown and weeds inhabited the gaps between the paving. In places, the bricks of the walls were coming loose. Gwen felt the deep stirring of some lost emotion. Too much had gone wrong really since, and now she had a young boy of her own, back in Hampstead. She had promised her husband Michael to be back by the end of the week. Edmund stood nearby in the archway, using it as a meagre shelter, as she went over to the sundial. It was wet and mossy, and of course, with it being so overcast, gave no shadow. Still, according to the journal, and what Massey had learned out in the Babylonian temples ... she took hold of the dial and rotated the metal disc one notch, then looked over to the door. Several minutes passed. Edmund was just about to say something when there was a knock.

"Hello," said Tony. Edmund fainted.

They all sat in a cafe, somewhere near the park on Gnaffid. Tony and two Gwendolines and Lord Massey III and poor Edmund, who looked around bewildered and mumbled to himself. Four versions of Tibbles scampered around the foot of the table.

"So, I'm a ... Clone?" said Gwen. "I'm not sure I'm familiar with the term."

"A copy of me," said Gwendoline. "Sort of like a twin, but one we make for ourselves. It was necessary to account for my absence you see, while I went off exploring."

"And the Tibbles, they are .."

"Clones too, yes. We have Tibbles Junior, Mr Tibbles, Tibbles the third, and McTibbles, who is actually an android. And whenever one pops its clogs, we just make a new one, so we never run short.."

"I see," said Gwen, who was not sure she did and was also uncertain how she felt about being a copy. "And Tony?"

"Well, I'm not sure we've forgiven him quite yet, for the naughtiness he managed all that time ago. What do you say, darling?"

She turned to Lord Massey, or Walter, as he insisted on being called.

"Worse things happen at sea dear," he said. "The Gnaffids are just scamps really."

"I suppose so. Do you remember the Vortles? Now weren't they horrid?"

"Quite glad their planet imploded to be honest. Although I wish we'd got hold of that Mesmotron."

"Next time darling, faint heart and all that .." There was a lull.

"So you have children?" Gwendoline asked.

"One boy, George. In London."

"We have two, back in the 1700s. Agnes and Henry. Splendid things really. They don't know about the garden."

"So, you go back and forth, whenever you want?"

"No, only at certain times."

"And what are you planning now?"

"Well .. I'd like you to take my place for a while. I want to take a look at the twentieth century, see how it panned out."

"Not too well, to be honest."

"Oh ... and well, I missed mama and papa of course."

"You missed them both, papa by three weeks, and mama by six years."

"Her turns?"

"Yes."

"Ah well, not to worry. Generally, these things can be ironed out .. is that not so darling?"

"Most of the time," said Walter. "Although it pays not to be complacent."

"Excuse me," said Edmund, and got up from the table. "I think I'll go and look around." He looked like a man trying to adjust to being in a dream, but wondering why it refuses to make those familiar bizarre missteps of logic. Gwen reached out to stop him but Gwendoline caught her by the wrist. "Leave him," she said. "It's best he gets used to things." They all watched him walk to the park. Furry birds flew over his head, their propellers whirring and the moons spun in the sky overhead.

Gwen walked with Walter to his spaceship, which was parked near the edge of the city. Looking at the craft she was mildly pleased to see that messieurs Wells and Verne had not been too far out with their imagineerings. Apart from that, she was worried about Gwendoline and Edmund.

"Do you think they'll be alright over there?" she asked Walter.

"Oh, they'll turn up trumps if Gwennie has anything to do with it. The important thing is they go soon, because the conjunction is about to close. As for us, I know another spot near Spaffel we can travel from. That links to the Munchausen place and we'll have to hope they kept the garden up. They tend to be rather sloppy about these things, and we have business in Austria."

"Edmund. Edmund." Her brother was still in a daze. He shook his head and looked around.

"Where are we?" he asked.

"In the peachery. You dozed off silly."

"The p .. what are we doing here?"

"I don't know. Scrumping maybe?"

"W-we need to get back, sort out fathers things."

"Why would we need to do that?"

"Need? Well, the funeral of course and the mess the estate is in." The day was still grey and rainy, and the trees of the orchard were bare, making Gwendoline's talk of scrumping nonsense.

"Oh Edmund," she said. "You must have been having quite the dream." She went over to the door and knocked. Her father answered the door. He was dressed in a souwester and carried a basket of wet foliage. He looked surprised.

"Gwennie!" he exclaimed. "And Edmund. What on earth are you doing in there?"

"Scrumping according to Edmund."

"Well, you're fortunate to catch me. I was just gathering some decoration for the dinner table .. the party your mother is throwing. And Edmund .. your brother is coming down from Edinburgh. He's looking forward to seeing you."

"It's damn fine to see you papa." Gwendoline rushed forward and threw her arms around him, kissing him on both cheeks. Her eyes were shiny, wet with tears.

"Gwennie!! What's got into you?" Still he was pleased. "You both better come inside. The chilly air has sent you both quite doolally." And with that they made their way out of the garden and went up to the house.

It was winter and snow fell on the estate. Edmund was still trying to come to terms with having dreamt the past ten years of his life. That is .. the version he remembered hadn't happened, and what had happened .. he had no memory of at all. This caused concern among his family as you might imagine and doctors were called. The only person unperturbed was Gwendoline, who said: if the version of reality he dreamt up, with its terrible war and the deaths of mother, father and William, was so awful, perhaps it were better to be here and now. That was before she went back to London, and now Edmund, fortunately a confirmed bachelor, was staying on at the estate. The gaps in his memory continued to disturb him, and in an attempt to make sense of them he began to go down to the walled garden, where he developed a habit of staring suspiciously at the door connecting the garden to the peachery. And it was while he was sat there, having cleared the snow off the bench, staring, that the knock came. He was alert all at once, but it was natural to hesitate. Everyone did.

"Come in." he said.

Houses

The blue house stood in the middle of some fields. It was visible from the lane that passed by the woods, then to get there, you drove down the farm track until you reached the gate. The area outside the house had been tarmaced and this was where we parked, pulling up outside the house in our Ford Capri. I rummaged around in the glove compartment until I found the house keys and then we got out of the car and walked over to the building. It was a bright and clear mid spring day.

Inside the house things were much as we had left them. Only some cups had been taken out of a kitchen cupboard and placed on the table. I looked at them. The dregs of three coffees, one white, two black. I took the cups over to the sink, rinsed them and placed them back in the cupboard. James had gone upstairs. He found a rumpled sleeping bag in the spare room, which he gathered up and placed back in the airing cupboard. An ashtray lay on the floor holding ash and half a dozen cigarette butts, alongside an empty wine bottle. The bottle we put in the dustbin outside along with the contents of the ashtray, which was washed under the outdoor tap and taken back to the car by James, while I locked the front door. Then I joined him in the car, taking my place in the driver's seat, and threw the keys back in the glovebox. I turned the car round and we drove out of the gate.

I woke up in the sleeping bag. There was the empty bottle of wine and the ashtray beside me. Some cold winter light filtered through the window of the spare room. I went to the bathroom to wash my face and relieve myself, then went downstairs. I could hear music coming from the kitchen. Cassandra had turned the radio on and made coffee. Peter was sat at the table, bleary eyed, drinking from his mug. I sat down besides him, and Cassandra brought two more mugs over, while the radio played Where Did Our Love Go. I saw that my coffee was black.

"I didn't know if you took milk," said Cassandra.

"Black is fine," I replied.

"Good time last night?"

"I must have. What happened to Elaine?"

Cassandra and Pete looked at each other. "She had to go," Peter said eventually.

We reached the red house later that day. It was on a cleared patch of ground in the middle of an industrial area. I parked up outside and took the keys from the glove compartment. We checked the house, it was clear, so we crossed the road and went over to the office block. It was dusk nearly, so the building would be empty. I found the right key and unlocked the entrance and we went into the lobby, heading straight for the elevator. It took us up to the third floor, then we stepped into the corridor and turned left, walking until we found door sixteen. I opened it and looked inside. The far wall was all window and down below across the road you could see the cleared patch of ground with the red house and the fabrication units that surrounded it. James went into the small office and put the ashtray back on the desk. Then he opened up a filing cabinet and flicked through the files until he found the orange one, marked 'O.S.I'.

"This is the one we need," he said.

I nodded and held the door open for him, as he took the file, closed the cabinet and went out. Then I followed him to the elevator and we left the building.

The next day I left the house and walked over to the office building. It was a rainy autumn morning. I said good morning to Louise on reception and took the elevator up to the third floor, then went to my office. The rain pattered against the window and then slid down the glass. Down below and across the road I could see the red house. I liked to see it down there, it was comforting. Someone had brought back my ashtray at long last, that was good. I took out my cigarettes, had a smoke then opened up the filing cabinet and looked for the orange file. It was missing. Where the hell was it? I flicked through all the files then checked the other drawers. It was gone. I started to panic.

We drove all night until we reached the yellow house on the coast. It was dawn by the time we arrived. It stood right on the beach, separated from the row of terraces and holiday lets behind it by a road. We parked and crossed the sand, passing by the side of the house to get to the front door. I unlocked the door while James turned away to look at the sea, the file under his arm. The waves rolled in and out the way they do. We went inside and wiped the sand off our shoes on a doormat in the hallway. Sand and small stones had gathered in small drifts along one wall. We went into the living room where there was a red sofa. I found the kitchen and started making cups of tea while James sat down and read the file. I came back through and placed two mugs on a low table in front of the sofa and sat down next to him.

"What does it say?" I asked.

"That he'll be here shortly," said James.

"We best get started then."

James nodded, so I went back to the car, opened up the boot and took out the bag and a length of rope. I looked at the sea. It rolled in and it rolled out again. I closed the boot and went back to the house.

Unit 2

A few days after the funeral, the envelope came through my letterbox. It was slightly bulky, so I shook it and there was a muffled jangling. I opened it up. There was a set of keys inside, and a letter from Colin's solicitors. I had no idea that Colin had solicitors. I took the letter with me to the kitchen and read it while I waited for the kettle to boil.

It read to the effect: that in the event of anything untoward occurring, Colin had entrusted me with the contents of the lock up he had rented, the one next to the viaduct. Why me, I had no idea. Colin was divorced: there was a son in Chester and a daughter in Leeds, but it seemed like this was a matter outside of the family. We did the occasional bit of business together: I sold him the odd piece of tribal crafts I found on the markets or in the antique shops. He was especially interested in under the counter juju, and I started to suspect this was the reason he had entrusted me with this post mortal endeavour. I was by nature, discreet.

I drove down to the viaduct. The lock up was one of three units on a cleared weedstrewn patch of ground. It was no.2. I unlocked it and let the shutter slide up. Inside there was an old armoire, four Goodyear tyres, two crates -the kind used by greengrocers - and a rusty sackcart propped in a corner. I went to look inside the crates: the top one contained eggs, large ones, about the size of my head, a blueish colour, speckled, packed in straw. I lifted off the top crate and placed it on the floor and looked at the one underneath. One egg, large, leathery, prehistoric. It pulsated gently. There was an invoice stapled to the side of the crate so I tore it off and read it: for Dixon, goods received, Benduni. No, it didn't make sense.

My curiosity wetted I went over to the armoire. In the top drawer was a framed photograph. Colin in Paris, the Eiffel Tower in the background. He had his arms around a pigeon, a large one, the size of himself. It was worrying. Pigeons generally were small and went around scavenging leftovers. I wondered if his wife had known and this had been the cause of his divorce.

In the second drawer down were some old paperbacks - science fictiony stuff by the look of them: Subliminal Vectors, The Lady in the Lake. I picked up Subliminal Vectors and flicked through. What the hell? Something about Dixon, Benduni .. I flicked further

"A few days after the funeral, the envelope came through my letterbox. It was slightly bulky .."

What the hell? Fuck fuck fuck. For some reason I went to the door of the unit and looked outside. All was normal. I went back inside. The only other thing in the armoire was an old ashtray in the bottom drawer and an orange file. Inside were some adverts that had been cut out of a magazine and paperclipped together, all featuring the same model. I took all these items outside and put them in the boot of my car. Where to begin with all this? Benduni was the least common name, I guess you started there. And Gatling St, that was a clue.

The A-Z was abandoned when I found it. Although the sign still hung outside, a To Let poster had been pasted to the inside of the window. Inside was an empty dusty space, all the old racks disassembled and stacked against a wall. From what I'd read of the story, maybe that was for the best. I took the number of the letting agent and made some enquiries about Benduni, explaining I had come into possession of some items that belonged to him. They agreed to pass on my number.

Several days later I got a message on my phone. I was relieved, not least because the large egg, which was stored with the rest of the items in my garage, had started to develop some hairline cracks and seemed to be on the verge of hatching. The message asked me to take ALL the items and drive to the parking lot next to the nearby reservoir, where somebody would meet me, take them off my hands and remunerate me for my troubles.

When I arrived at the reservoir there was one other car waiting. It was early, scarcely six am, and the sun was low and weak over the hills and the wind was cold. It was an E type jaguar with a woman leaning against the door on the drivers side wearing a headscarf and tweed jacket. She introduced herself as Gwendoline. I hesitated.

"Not Gwendoline from the story?" I asked. She looked as though she could be, and her accent was clipped, aristocratic.

"Probably," she sighed. "Although really, who the fuck knows by this stage."

"In that case," I said. "I don't want money."

"You don't?" she said, taking a cigarette from her handbag. She lit it and looked at me. "Ah, I suppose .."

"I want to see the garden."

"Of course you do." She grinned. "Good for you."

I transferred the items to the boot of her own vehicle, then got back in my car and prepared to follow her.

The Lady in the Lake

It was an obscure art gallery on the fringes of town, a converted mill. I'm not sure even, how the flyer came into my possession. One of those things you find in your jacket pocket after a night out. I must have been between jobs and in the doldrums, and on an impulse decided to go instead of what? looking out of the window at the rain.

So I went to the exhibition. It could not be said it was popular. Apart from the bored art graduate manning the entrance, there was only one other punter, and I suspected him of being a homeless gentleman come in from the downpour. But I was there so I looked around. It was much as I feared, half ass conceptual - a chair stuck upside down to the ceiling with tinsel hanging off it, multiculturalism - still - jesus, wasn't everyone fed up of it by now? It was hard to shake the feeling, it was just a way for the well heeled to find a career for their more useless kids. Read the accompanying thesis - no, fuck you.

Then though, there was the last gallery I entered, on the top floor. It was a video installation, the room darkened. I sat down with a feeling of trepidation, what pointlessness I was going to have to suffer through next. The video started somehow as soon as I sat down, projected onto the wall opposite. Flickers. A face out of focus, cut off by the edge of the camera, one eye open in alarm ... dread. Planets floated in the background. The voice started, female, filtered, as though transmitted from far far away:

" .. i live in a drowned world, all i see are shapes in ripples

i am held by weeds, do not let me freeze "

Flickers, a lake, reeds around the edges, a tower in the background. Ripples over the lake, something reflected from up above, out of shot, monstrous like a cloud of eyeballs, absorbing and expelling each other. My fingernails dug into the chair. A bare room, two masked figures sit there on chairs, one against each wall, one male one female. They do not speak. There is one window above the male figure. Something is clawing at it. The video ends and I exhale. I do not move for a while, after which I realise my fingernails are embedded in the chair. I pull them loose and stand up quickly, knocking the chair over and back out of the room. I do not feel right, but that is okay. I am aware that something meaningful has happened.

Down by the entrance I ask the graduate for the name of the artist, email if he's got it. He is grateful of course for the opportunity to do something, but not having been given a business card is obliged to consult a ledger. He scrawls down the details for me on the back of my notebook: Rachel Galloway c/o pescopesco@jmd.com.

"Do you know her?" I ask.

He screws up his face. "Not reaaalllly.. " he says. "I met her on opening night. She was .. hard to talk to."

That seemed to be it. I went back outside where it was still raining. Just for a moment there seemed to be two masked figures watching me from across the street, but then a bus went past and obscured them and then they were gone.

I got a reply to my email two days later. I had written something vague - intrigued by the video, how did you make it, would love to meet - and so was surprised to get an address straight away. Northpoint Studios, etc, etc. - present Thursday afternoons. It wasn't too many miles away, a neighbouring town. I drove over the next day.

The studio, like the gallery, was part of some converted industrial building. There were buzzers by the entrance, and one was labelled 'Northpoint S', the writing lazily scrawled in blue biro. I buzzed, twice, then someone answered, Rachel as it transpired.

"Carl, I sent the email," I said.

"Third floor," she said. The buzzer buzzed and I went in, a cold concrete landing, pipes running along the walls. Stone steps with a cranky wooden bannister. I followed them upwards. Each landing was stacked with something, old signs, shelving struts, guttering. On the third floor I pushed open the heavy wood door and went in. The space was good, large industrial windows along one side, cubicles constructed from hardboard along the other, a communal space with a long table down the middle. There were canvases propped up against walls, tubes of paint on the table, boxes of materials. Metal cans, the smell of white spirit. Someone was working in a cubicle, I could hear the muffled sound of reggae from a radio. Rachel was waiting for me by the table. She was in her late twenties, the face of a serious practical person, dressed in a cardigan, jeans and trainers. We shook hands.

"Do you paint as well?" I asked.

"Sometimes .. I used to," she replied vaguely. "Lately, just videos."

"Why?"

"I find the footage, it seems important that I use it."

"You find it. Can I ask .. where?"

"Some of it is mine, the rest gets posted to me."

"Right. You mean .. a collaboration?"

She nodded. "Mm hh. Look." She went to one of the boxes on the table, one that was stuffed with cables and wiring, an old vcr, a keyboard, and took out a dogeared paperback book. She handed it to me and I looked at the cover: The Lady in the Lake by Roland McKinley. By the condition, artwork and printed price, it had to be twenty years old.

"That guy," she explained, "he sends me stuff, on old videotapes, I have to convert it."

"Right. And how did you meet him?"

"Same way you met me. I read the book and got in touch."

I leafed through the book. It was on Pan, usually a good sign, and looked like a fantasy novel or historical fiction maybe:

"i strode towards the tower, it stood against the blank mirror sky with its moons, all staring at me. the lake ripples, it ripples always. Is Palimere down there?"

"God," I said. "Where did you find this?"

"The bargain table in a second hand bookshop. You can look online, you won't find a copy anywhere. A couple of other books by the author, non fiction. Eventually, I spoke to someone who worked for Pan - she remembered, there was a run of about a hundred and then it was ditched. Too many complaints."

"Complaints. What about?"

"They said: you don't read the book, the book reads you."

I laughed. "And what does Roland say about that?"

"We never spoke. I sent him a letter through .. Barbara, I think it was .. told him how affecting the book was, that I was a painter/video artist and the tapes started arriving."

"You weren't tempted to go see him?"

She shook her head. "I just know, if I do that, the tapes stop coming," she said.

"You're still getting them?"

"Now and again, less frequently." She flipped open a battered old laptop that was on the table next to her. Turned it on and opened a folder on the desktop. I watched the video. It was the tower again, from a different angle, the lake behind it. Wind blew the grasses, you could hear the noise it made. Somewhere offscreen there was a screaming. It was unnerving, but Rachel just watched, fascinated. I was glad when she turned it off.

"It's amazing work," I said. "Its the only thing that matters."

She looked at me and we understood each other.

"Yes," she said, relieved. "Thank you."

"Will you give me his address?"

She sighed. Then went back to the crate of cables and pulled out an envelope. She removed the letters inside and handed it to me. The address was on the front - Dorset. She looked at me again, but more sadly this time.

"There you go," she said.

I took it, apologised, and left the studio.

I drove down to Dorset the next day. It took four hours, then an hour to find the village mentioned on the envelope. It was quaint, the kind you see on TV. McKinley had a cottage, thatched what else, but I laid odds he wasn't a farmer or that locals owned anywhere near half the properties in the village anymore. I pulled up outside. Had it been foolish to just turn up? Why the fuck should he talk to me anyway? Still, I was here. I went over to the cottage, opened the gate and down the garden path to the front door.

Half an hour later I was sat in Mckinley's front room talking to him. He was in his fifties, crumpled slacks and cardigan, reading glasses, your stereotypical reclusive author. We were sharing a pot of tea.

"That book, yes, a disaster," he said. "It's my non fiction keeps me afloat and the odd periodical. My account of the Hundred Years War is considered something of a touchstone among historians."

"But the book, what started that?" I asked.

"Oh, it was a transcription of a much older manuscript, non canon Arthurian. French author, but working from a Welsh source - Simone de Montpassant, 12th century. Like I said, never found its way into the canon, too fucking weird. Lucky to find it at all really. The Bibliotheque Nationale dug it out of the back room of a monastery, no other copies. And he was working, so he claimed from the Green Book of Gwlwlyd, which there's never been a mention of anywhere else, so .."

"So what about the videos," I said, eventually.

"Ah yes." He stared at the floor. "Well, I was always a bit of a home video nut, when I was married with the kids. They don't talk to me now. But the manuscript had marginalia, and then the people turned up, they agreed to take me .."

"People?" He was beginning to ramble.

He looked up sharply over the top of his glasses. "Yes," he said. "You know the ones I'm talking about."

I did. We looked at each other. "Where did they take you?" I asked.

I was getting ready to leave when Mckinley came into the room with a pink cardboard folder. It was stuffed with notes, postcards, paperclipped sheets of A4 lined. He took out a photograph. "That's from the Louvre," he said, "unknown artist, Rococo period." I looked at it. It was the tower and lake from the videos, similar, but the lake was frozen. You could see the woman trapped underneath and two moons in the sky. Strange things reflected in the ice from above, like eyes, if you cared to notice.

"We're not the first," he said.

I left the cottage and got into my car. It was late afternoon, drizzly, autumn, and some way to Gwlwlyd. When I got there it was evening. I, some said foolishly, didn't use a smartphone and hadn't booked a place to stay, and the time when you could arrive at a town and find a hotel with a room to spare seemed to have passed. There wasn't much wandering any more, we were all being prepackaged. I parked outside the railway station and watched the rain make the flagstones all wet. The last train had arrived and left some time ago and now there weren't even any taxis waiting. I dozed a little, then woke up a bit groggy. It was morning and across the way the masked man and the masked woman were sat on a bench near the taxi rank and the birds were singing. I blinked and rubbed my eyes and then it was still evening and everywhere was drizzly and deserted again.

Morning came and even though it was still raining, I went for a look around the town. It was famous for its Norman castle mainly. Down by the old market a cafe was open and I had breakfast and coffee, then the shops started opening and people started arriving for work and I found the library and went into the local history section. This was a small room lined with solid wooden bookshelves, above which on one wall was a row of small windows. There were long tables in the centre and a couple of computers on which were stored archive material. The librarian acknowledged me as I entered, and I started by reading about the castle. As I suspected, the hill it had been built on was the site of a fort well before the Norman age, before even the Saxons and Romans, the seat of power for some ancient Britonic tribe. Some arthurian scholars even speculated it was the site of one of his eleven battles, before routing the Saxons at Badon.

I started reading one of the most outspoken proponents of this theory, a local historian, unfortunately deceased, named William Harris. It was in his slim self published 1930s monograph - local myths and folklore of Gwlwlyd, an oral tradition - that I read the accounts of a tower that had once been on the hill, of the chieftain who had found the lady in the lake, of the curse that followed 'when the tower had been swallowed by moons'. All this, the author asserted without proof, as written in the G.B. I flicked through the book in an effort to find an account of his references, but at the back was only the simple statement

- *'we have come now to take you to Palimere'.*

I looked up and saw that I was alone in the library. The librarian was somehow absent. There was a tapping above me, and I looked up and for an instance saw a claw at one of the small windows. I felt a dreadful chill. I had an awareness, if I left the room there would be something different outside. Not the rest of the library, not even the town of Gwlwyld but just a big lake perhaps with the moons circulating above it and the eyes submerged underneath. The lady in the lake stood at the entrance to the room. Her mask moved.

Rachel Galloway leaves the mill containing her studio and goes to the bus shelter. The man is waiting for her.

"Do we have to?" she asks.

"Yes," he says.

They get on the bus and go home.

Zodiac

Capricorn

In the beginning everything was unformed. You might describe it as a mist or a swamp or some combination of the two, and there was water all around.

Aquarius

At some point, something fluttered past and laid an egg in the water and that egg was the moon. It cracked open and out slid the sun like a huge yolk on an effluvial river of stars. Half the moon stayed where it was and the sun took the other half and used it as a boat to float down the river. The sun and the moon had offspring, although it was unclear to us, at first, what we were meant to do. Then a great fish swam up out of the waters and told us that we should dig a river, just like the river of stars and when we did this the channel filled with fresh water and the freshest water was at the centre and this was where we lived.

Pisces

The great fish was watching us all the while and then it gave birth to a second fish that swam up the new river and from itself produced sorcerous monsters: howling giants that brought thunder and lightning and breathed molten fire or covered everything with ice. Then the sun came across the river on his boat. The sun had two faces, one that faced forward and one that faced backwards, so that he could see where he was going and where he had come from and now he said that the first fish should be gutted so that an arch could be constructed from its bones and then its skin be stretched over to make a firmament which would protect us from the deluges up above. Once this was done, our murky waters settled until a mountain of land appeared. Then the celestial river was raised above the earthly river so that it pivoted around the axis of the mountain. Then four gates were constructed, two above, two below, so that the sun could sail between heaven and earth. Finally it ordered that the second fish be castrated so that it create no more monsters. Its seed was then spread across the land to make a garden, and the genitals were thrown into the waters and from this was born a magnificent bird that flew upwards to the far bank of the starry river above. The bird coupled with the sun to make many celestial daughters, who drew water from the starry river and made a beautiful golden garden of their own filled with light, so beautiful that I longed to go there, and so the sun came back over the river in his boat and offered to ferry me to the far embankment.

I stayed there for a while and spent delightful hours, but then I looked back across the river and saw that the castrated fish had shed its scales to become a woman. So I asked to return and once again the twin faced sun took me across the river. The bird in the garden had dropped its feathers to become a woman also. This was bright Venus and she closed the gates behind me, saying that from now on only the sun might be permitted to pass through and that the fish Lilith, who was to become my wife, would be the messenger between heaven and earth, and that when heaven was pleased she would call for rain but when it was angered dry winds would be summoned to harrow the land. Upon my return, in imitation of the celestial gardens above, I supervised the construction of new canals, so that around the mountain were reedbeds and meadows. Then it was that I was declared king and I wore great antlers upon my head as a crown.

The time came when my wife bore a daughter Eve. She was as incandescent and alluring as the moon, and one morning she was on the riverbank when the sun sailed by on his boat. He turned the first of his faces towards her and offered to take her across to the golden garden.

"But we shall be seen," said Eve.

"No," said the ferryman, "for if you were to ask, the moon would hide her face, and all here tonight would be dark."

So when the night was dark they went over to the golden garden and made love, so that Eve was with child.

"And now what should I do?" she asked.

The ferryman went over to a tree and picked a fruit.

"Take this as a gift for your father, for the fruit is an intoxicant," he said "and then while he lies inebriated, allow the pair of you to be discovered in a state of nakedness and tell how you were seduced. Then shall your father be shamed and the child people believe you have conceived be made king in his stead."

And this seemed to Eve a very good plan.*

*there is another version of this tale, where I was indeed intoxicated and slept with my daughter, and the resulting child was so monstrous I decided to eat it, but it continued to grow inside me, and I had to be castrated or decapitated or *planted so it could be birthed, but this is so unpleasant to recall, I decided to omit it from this account.*

After all this had occurred Lilith ordered us to be banished from the mountain, and as warned, sent not rain but dry winds instead so that the land was parched and meagre and the people toiled to survive.

The land needed a new king so the sun ferried the child over to the far bank and asked Venus to make a fire and bake the child so he was hard like a clay pot, and this she did, dangling him over the flames so that all was burnt except for a spot on the ankle where she held him and when the firing cracked the child was impervious.

Then when the sun was ferrying the child back across the river he spied Lilith waiting for them and a new notion occurred to him. He gave the child his staff which he used to steer the boat and named him the new sun, and once ashore took Lilith for himself and declared that he was Lord of the mountain. Then he blocked the channels so that all the fresh water still available was stored inside the mountain and the waters outside were briny.

Angered, Venus closed the gates between the two rivers and the child Kenan was unable to sail across the sky and his boat drifted until it became marooned on the dry bank of the canal. Then it was dark and very cold. That was when he went among the women and they raised a race of giants, whom he taught the secret of fire as he had seen it in the garden, and they began to hunt and feast on the people, who they called animals and so they learned to survive in the wilderness, and to his mother Eve he gave the animal hides so she learned to make clothes to keep warm and cover her nakedness.

Then Lilith gave birth to a child from the time when we were together and he was called Jared, but she told the sun that the boy was his so that he might be spared. The sun however, favouring Kenan, refused to believe her and ordered the child to be served up for dinner, this being the new way of things. And so Lilith took a piece of the mountain and carved a facsimile of the child from stone and served it up to the sun wrapped in swaddling and Jared she hid deep within the mountain.

Now, wishing to honour Kenan without revealing his lineage, the sun lauded praise upon the mighty hunter and invited him to the mountain to serve as attendant and cupbearer, but before he left embittered Eve gave Kenan a similar fruit to the one with which she had intoxicated her father and whispered in his ear how he might restore water to the people.

In the mountain, Kenan saw the pools of water that the sun had hoarded and was angered, so once invited to serve the sun in his bathing chamber he took the chalice and mixed the water with the juice of the fruit he'd been given to make beer. In the chamber he spied his father's nakedness and served him until he was drunk, so drunk that he spewed up the stone he had eaten and caused it to shatter into shards. Kenan took up one of these shards, leapt into the water and used it to hack off his father's genitals. The sun fought back savagely, but unable to wound the flesh of the child he had baked in the fire, succeeded only in gouging out one of his eyes. Hearing the commotion Lilith entered the chamber to see the carnage and blood drenched waters and ran out but Kenan pursued her into the bedchamber.

Then Kenan released the waters, which came out as a great flood, but having learnt the secret of stone, Kenan took the boulders which the deluge wrenched from the land and used tools to carve them into great mountain valleys which channelled the waters into a river. And this river was the Nile which left the land of Kush and went into Egypt and Libya.

Aries

Now one day out from the mountain on this river floated a coracle made of reeds and in it was baby Jared and it drifted until it caught in the roots of a willow. Eve was walking by the river when she heard the babes cries and so she rescued it and brought it to me at our house by the sea where Eve had learnt how to tame some of the animals and so he was raised by her among the shepherds.

Then Kenan came down to the sea. He had killed a lion while hunting and Eve made him a robe out of the skin so that the head of it covered his own and concealed his scarred face and missing eye. He took the severed genitals of his father and threw them into the sea and then the gates between heaven and earth reopened and Venus appeared and where she walked grew grasses and flowers and the land was fertile.

On the mountain had been born from Lilith Kenan's son Mahalel and Kenan stated his desire that Mahalel should be king and marry Venus, while he once more took up the role of the sun and sailed the boat across the heavens. So it was he took up his staff and the shell of the moon and sailed across the starry river, while below the wedding took place, for which Mahalel invented music and dancing and devised the rhythms of the seasons and the lads and maidens all danced by the river with flowers in their hair.

Gemini

Still the rains were not sent and so Venus ventured down into the underworld, where Lilith and Set had been imprisoned by Kenan underneath the mountains. There she learnt from her sister of Kenan, from where he was born and of Mahalel also and how Jared was the rightful king, and that the rains would not come unless he was set over the people.

And so Venus went to Jared, who during this time had become the dearest friend of Mahalel, for while Mahalel was to the people like a shepherd and protector unto his flock, Jared was strong like a bull and dug the canals and made the meadows and pastures, but when Venus showed herself to him he was unable to do anything but believe her words and full of resentment went to see his friend.

"Know that you are my brother," he said and then picked up a rock and smashed in his head and beat him until it was crushed and the gore went into the ground.

And when Mahalel's sisters saw what had happened they cried and cried and it rained and did not stop for many days.

Taurus

Jared then went to Kenan and for many days they wrestled and fought so that the earth shook, and still the rain fell so that everything was a chaos. Lilith had sent the winds and storms to assist Jared but still he could not defeat the giant. Then Venus brought him the knife of flint that had been used to castrate Set and told him of how Kenan had been baked in the fire except for his ankle, and so Jared ducked low and severed the giant's tendon so that he fell helpless to the ground.

Then Jared took from Kenan the lionskin and sent him into exile, and that he was known by his limp and missing eye none would give him shelter.

Cancer

Still it continued to rain and the waters rose and rose, and ...

I'm pausing in my account here because it occurs to me that some of you will have heard other tales of Jared, such as how he fought the water snake and got caught by the ankle himself and had his sinews and eyes taken, but as the new culture hero taking over from the previous one these tales are .. how should I say .. borrowed from his predecessor and I see no value in regurgitating them here

and they continued until the land could no longer be distinguished from the sea so I found the shell of a giant crab or maybe a turtle and we gathered together all we could and floated until we could see that nearly the whole world had been covered by the deluge. Then a bird appeared up above and guided us towards the last piece of land which was the peak of the mountain emerging from the waters like a solitary island and so we let loose the few surviving animals, and climbed to the top and there were Lilith and the seven sisters still weeping and unable to stop even though the water was now lapping around their ankles.

"They will not cease," Lilith said, "I cannot make them."

There was not much to be done except take the sisters and hold their heads under the water until they drowned and then we let the sea take them. Then the waters settled and we sat down and waited for them to recede.

Leo

And Jared took to wearing the lionskin and became king and like his predecessor gathered the rocks to channel the waters, only this time the rivers were the Tigris and the Euphrates and stone temples were built at the points to which the highest floodwaters had risen.

Virgo

And the lands around the rivers: Lydia, Aram, Assyria, Meshech and Elam, Jared granted to Venus where she taught the people how to plant seed and make the land fertile and grow crops, and then to Jared's consternation, she flew away.

Libra

And around the fields grew cities and Lilith served as the Oracle and determined matters of justice, so that when people erred the river snake would recede back into the mountains and the land would become fallow. Then with law and agriculture came writing and I knew our time was coming to an end.

One of these laws was that Eve, of whom she was jealous, stay chaste and remain in the wilderness. It was here that Kenan, impervious to the flood and wandering in exile, spied his mother and attempted to ravage her (although some would say that this was actually Jared wearing the lionskin) and anyway she struggled so he only succeeded in brushing against her leg and ejaculating onto the ground, and from this seed grew a tree and from this tree emerged Mahalel born again.

Then hearing of the new lands Kenan went into the cities and this time he was welcomed for he taught them new tricks with fire, how to make tools and weapons from metal, and the people fell into war. Even Jared welcomed him into the mountain where he chained up the Oracle and took charge of her temples and her priestesses were sacrificed on horned altars.

Scorpio

So that one day while Kenan was resting, Lilith sent a scorpion up through a crevice in a rock to sting him on the ankle and he died. Mahalel found him and exchanged the lyre he had made for Kenan's staff and then lay him on a boat and set it adrift upon the river and Venus heard the wind make wonderful music on the strings of the lyre and opened the gate and let him pass into the heavenly garden, the first man to ever enter since myself all those countless million years ago.

Sagittarius

The staff of Mahalel was fashioned as a serpent wrapped around a tree, for both of these are the symbol of the river and also the symbol of the serpent Set who now guards the gate into the garden. And it was said for the land to prosper the king must sacrifice a child of his own and Mahalel would lead this child through the underworld and past the serpent into the garden beyond to become the new sun. And to convince the people of this he gave them wine and gold and weapons of iron and horses on which they came down from Scythia into Europe and India. That though, is a whole new story.

Part Three
The Idle King

Doppelganger

I was backing out of a layby when another white van came around the corner and ran into mine. The two vans were virtually identical except for the writing on the side, and when the driver of the other vehicle got out I saw he was also so identical to me as to be a replica. Really, it was like looking in a mirror, and the only difference between us was his strong Welsh accent.

"Bloody hell, man," he said, "Look before you pull out will you."

And I know you're not supposed to admit you're at fault, because of the insurance and everything, but really, who can live like that?

"Yes sorry," I said, "I got distracted."

This appeased him to some extent. "Well okay," he said, "but look at the state of my fender, how are we going to square this?"

"You want to swap insurance details?" I asked hesitantly. He demurred, and I got the impression that like myself, he was on less than straight terms with the insurance company. He looked instead at the side of my van.

"Paul, landscaper and handyman," he read out loud. "Well, I'll tell you what. The wife has been on at me for ages to sort out the garden. You go live at mine, spend a month fixing it up, and we'll call it quits." This seemed reasonable.

"And where are you going to stay in the meanwhile?" I asked.

"Your house of course," he said. "We'll swap vans and keys and no one will be any the wiser, and then I'll meet you here in a month's time."

So, that is exactly what we did. I put my landscaping gear in the back of his van - the side of which read 'Aaron - building and plumbing' - and he transferred his equipment to mine and then we swapped licence plates and were on our way.

It took me a couple of hours to drive down to his house, which was on the outskirts of a lovely Welsh village. Obviously, he'd done very well for himself - it was a charming stone cottage with a good size garden. Worth a pretty penny I imagined. His wife was called Fiona and she was very striking also. I told her that the van had been damaged and I was going to spend some time working on the garden which pleased her a lot. I went to look at the garden and saw it was indeed in a state. The grass was long and unkempt, the borders overgrown and filled with weeds, and I figured that the addition of a patio and rockery would make the place a whole lot nicer, so I looked up the phone numbers of some local suppliers and then started strimming the grass.

At the end of the first day, I went inside to a lovely meal that Fiona had cooked for me - roast duck, carrots and potatoes - then she asked me if I wanted to go to bed. This placed me in an awkward situation, as you might imagine.

"Not tonight," I said. "I think I'll sleep on the couch."

After a few nights of this, Fiona, understandably disgruntled, went to stay at her mothers. I kept on with my work regardless and by the end of the month the garden was looking great, if I do say so myself. The lawn was trimmed and neat, there were potted plants on the new stone patio, flowering shrubs and a young apple tree in the borders and alpines tucked into the crevices of the rockery. I admired it for a while then I packed away my gear and drove back to the junction where I'd run into Aaron, or was it that he'd run into me? He was waiting there anyway, leaning against his van.

"How did it go?" he asked.

"Fine," I said. "There was a misunderstanding with Fiona though, she went to stay at her mothers."

He seemed satisfied with this answer. "Don't worry about that," he said. "I'll sort it out when I get back." We shook hands and went our separate ways again.

When I got back to my own house, I found to my amazement it had been completely renovated, from top to bottom. The loose tiles on the roof had been replaced, the brickwork repointed and a new front door and windows fitted. It looked marvellous. There was even a fancy door knocker, the face of the Green Man with the ring of the knocker clasped between his teeth. It made me think: it was time I found a wife of my own, settled down.

I soon found a promising candidate. A very bonny lass if I might say so, one of those ethereal types. I started noticing her because she came past my house about the same time every week, just as I was getting ready to watch Match of the Day, then she would stop and stare at the window. At first, I thought she might be looking at me, but then I figured she must be admiring the building. It certainly stood out from the rest of the street, after all the work Aaron had done on it, and to complement his efforts, I had put up some hanging baskets and relaid the patio.

So naturally, I contrived so as to be outside at the time she next walked past, even though this meant missing some of Mr Linekars essential pre match analysis concerning the state of the various divisions. Instead, I got my toolbox and began tightening and oiling the hinges on the front gate (a job, to be fair, that needed doing anyway), and lo and behold, she started walking down the street towards me. I applied a bit more WD40 then looked up. She was still walking down the street, the same distance away. I frowned, then pointlessly loosened and tightened the bolts again. Then I looked back, she was still walking, the same distance away. That was strange. Eventually, I wiped my hands on a rag (normally, heh, I might have wiped them on my trousers), stood up and called down the street.

"Hello," I yelled. She started to get closer, but now I was committed of course. She was giving me an enigmatic look, somewhere between amusement and wariness if I had to describe it.

"Hello," I started again as she drew near. She was pale, blonde, rather enchanting. "I've ... noticed you pass by, you always look at the house, I was wondering why." Did that sound right? It had the virtue of being accurate. I smiled to signify it was an enquiry, not a demand.

She seemed nonchalant about the encounter anyway. "Just a feeling I had about the house," she said. "That door knocker maybe. Who put that there?"

"That? Oh, a friend of mine who did some work for me, his own personal touch. Do you live round here?"

"Nearby." The question made her more guarded. I saw that she shrank back inside herself.

"Just that you pass by often."

"I've moved here recently. I had some trouble back at home."

"Oh, I'm sorry to hear that. Well, if you need some help ..." I indicated the door knocker, "... finding your way around, er .. local services, that sort of thing .."

"Or if I get lonely."

"Well, yes that too." She wrinkled her nose fetchingly. "I know where you are .." she said, leaving the sentence open-ended.

"Paul," I added.

"Rhiannon," she said, and walked off down the street. I watched her for a few moments, then instinctively looked down and tested the gate and when I looked up again, she was gone.

Two weeks later, I was lucky enough to be in a restaurant with her on a date. She was telling me how she came to move here. There was a man of course - possessive, demanding.

"It can't work," she said, "but he doesn't see that."

"And you had to move all this way to escape from him?"

She nodded, chewing her food. Lamb with seasonal vegetables, which she held, pierced delicately on her fork, waiting for her next bite.

"What you need is someone to look after you," I said.

"I know, and then I had that feeling when I saw the house."

"Where are you living?"

"A flat. It's small but secure. Although I confess, there are times when I feel like a prisoner."

"Ah, that's no good. A woman like you is meant to be free, anyone can see that."

She swallowed and gave me a winning smile. "And you Paul, any ambitions?" she asked.

I thought about this. "Marriage. Maybe kids," I said. "Settle down a bit."

She nodded carefully. "That sounds okay," she said. I raised my glass and she rapped hers against it, with that strange expression again, somewhere between diffidence and amusement.

A few nights later, I was down at the Old Hen, watching 'winner stays on' at the dartboard. While I was waiting for my turn, I got talking to this man called Gordon. He was new, I hadn't seen him in here before. "Just passing through, a sales gig," he explained.

I noticed a hint of Welsh to his accent. I told him I'd been down that way not too long ago.

"Lovely countryside," I said. "Great scenery."

"Yeah, boring as fuck though innit?" he replied. "Better here."

"You think so?" I replied dubiously. My own small town had never really struck me as a social epicentre.

"Probably. Fuck, how the hell do I know? I suppose it's all the same old shit when it comes down to it." He seemed to be out of sorts. Whether that was due to circumstance or his natural temperament, it was hard to discern.

"Probably, yes."

I was glad to see I was up for the next game. I took on Trevor and managed to finish on a treble eighteen, beating him squarely. "Good arrows," he said, shaking my hand and then going to buy me an obligatory pint. Next, I was taking on Gordon.

"Want to make this interesting, Paul?" he asked.

"Interesting in what way Gordon?" I replied.

"To the tune of ten pounds. I've been watching your game and I reckon I can take you."

"Better men than you have tried and failed Gordon."

"Oh, you think so do you?"

"Yes, I do."

"Let's see the colour of your dubloons then, you knobwart."

We each tucked our ten pound notes behind the scoreboard and the game began. Gordon did well at first, hitting the trebles, but was less sure around the edges of the board. I managed to pip him by leaving myself a twenty to finish on.

"Fuckbastard!!!" he yelled. "Fucking fuckbastard. Dammit!!" He didn't take losing very well. I collected my winnings with a modest smile and just the right trace of superiority.

"Okay, another game, fifty quid this time," he announced.

"Winner stays on," I pointed out.

"Screw that," said Gordon, taking the notes out of his wallet and turning to address the punters who had been watching the game. "Rematch," he declared. "Hundred quid on the table. Anyone got a problem with that?" He seemed drunk, but then he'd been knocking back doubles as well as pints. No one had a problem anyway, or they were interested to see how the wager played out. This time I beat him by leaving myself with an easy hundred to finish on, while he languished on an awkward one one three.

"NOOOOOOO!! SHit your bastard fuck whore mother!!" he screamed. It seemed melodramatic, but anyway I'd had enough of it all by now, and I figured the hundred would allow me to take Rhiannon somewhere good: the ballet or one of those other things she liked. I took my winnings and held out my hand for him to shake.

"That's me done," I said. "Tough luck, it was a tight game."

"Ohhhhh no way. No fucking way," he responded. "Back on that board, I want to win my money back."

There was a murmur of disapproval from the people watching. This was obviously bad form, but there was a latent frisson of excitement too - the possibility of the stakes being raised even further.

"No," I said. "I won't bet anymore."

"Don't have to," he slurred, fishing around in his trouser pocket. He pulled out his car keys. "That's a Peaugot, up against the hundred you just won."

"Don't be ridiculous Gordon, you're drunk," I said, "I won't take it."

"Why not?"

"Because you're drunk."

"Don't tell me I'm drunk. You're drunk you fucking English pantyliner .. trying to make me look cheap in front of your pals .."

"Take it," someone yelled, I think it was Derek. There was a murmur of assent. "Teach the silly bastard a lesson," someone else added. There was laughter. Well, I guessed it would be amusing for someone to lose their car on a game of darts, and I'd give it back the next day of course. It would make a good story for the regulars.

By now, Gordon was too drunk even to hit high numbers from the off. I was under the magic one eighty while he was struggling to break three hundred. I polished matters off with two trebles and a double top. There was uproar in the pub, nearly everyone left in there having crowded round to watch the match. Gordon didn't even bother cursing, he just stormed out of the pub leaving his car keys behind. People moved out of his way. His face was like ruddy thunder.

I was woken up the next morning by the sound of my phone ringing on the dresser next to the bed. I felt groggy but not too hungover: able to blink myself to some semblance of waking, pick it up and answer.

"Happy, are you?" said a familiar Welsh tinged voice. I tried to place it. It took a short while for all the events of the previous evening to take up their properly allocated locations in my brain. Eventually I groaned, audibly, I think.

"Yes, exactly," Gordon said with a kind of malevolent glee. Evidently, he was the type of person who took satisfaction in his own misfortunes, as well as those of others. "Brand new Peaugot waiting for you to collect. How am I meant to get to my sales appointments now, eh?"

It occurred to me that I hadn't even wanted the bet in the first place and to be cast as the culprit in all this was rather unfair. But to go into all that was too tiring. Instead, I simply said, "Don't worry, I'll bring you the keys back, just tell me where."

"And tell everyone I welched on a bet, yeah?" Really, he was impossible.

"Up to you," I said, losing patience. I looked around at the discarded clothes lying at the foot of the bed, trying to spot a t shirt. I felt him simmer at the other end of the phone. "Meet me back at the pub at twelve," he said eventually.

I walked back into the Hen, ready to hand the keys over in a spirit of magnanimity, maybe even share a joke about it, only

120

to find him not stood at the bar or sat at any of the tables, but waiting by the dartboard. I had a sudden rotten feeling. There were no other customers, just the publican. I ordered a pint and went over.

"Right, what do you want me to put up now?" asked Gordon.

"Gordon," I answered. "You can have the car keys."

He shook his head. "Not good enough," he said. "I have my pride to think of. What is it you want?"

"I don't even know what you've got," I said.

He reflected on this. "That's true," he said. He fished in his other trouser pocket and pulled out a different set of keys. "My house," he said, "if you win. Otherwise, I take back what's mine."

"Fine," I said. Well, if the man was really prepared to lose his house, I was exasperated enough now by the ridiculous situation to let him. The hell with it.

"Say it," he said.

"You lose, I get the house. Otherwise, you take back what's yours."

"Brilliant," he said, "let's go."

I stepped up to the ockey and put away a quick one forty, but then Gordon came straight out with three treble twenties. He followed up next with treble nineteens, leaving him with the classic one fifty to finish. I fluffed my last dart, missing the double and leaving myself with two twenty one. Then he finished with treble twenty, double twenty and one dart dead centre.

"BULLSEYE!!"" he cried, "GET IN! YESSSSS! You dismal shitbasket!" It was gratifying to see he was as graceful in victory as defeat.

"Well done," I said wearily, and held out the keys.

"What's that?" he asked.

"Your car," I said, puzzled. "You just won it back."

"I wasn't talking about the car Paul."

"No?" I creased my brow. I was still, for some reason, holding out the keys. I reluctantly took them back. "What then?"

"Rhiannon of course."

I felt frozen. That is, nothing seemed to move for a while. "What do you mean Rhiannon?" My own voice sounded unconvincing to me.

"You know what I mean Paul. She's mine and I'm taking her back."

"But I was talking about the car."

"That's not what you said though is it? Where I come from, we say what we mean."

"You're the one she came here .. to get away from."

He didn't like that. "She didn't come here, she was sent," he said, "and anyway .. that's nothing to do with you. We set

122

terms and now you have to meet them, that's all there is to it."

He was right of course.

"What do you mean you lost me on a bet?!!" screamed Rhiannon. I noticed now that when she was angry, her own Welsh accent started to emerge.

"It was a mistake," I said. "Your ex boyfriend hustled me."

"Not Gordon? You made a bet with Gordon? Oh my Godd!!" Her tone was rising to a really intolerable pitch.

"I didn't know who he was. It was a grift."

"And he's outside now?"

"Err.." He was actually. I'd left him quite smug, leaning on the roof of the Peaugot, with the passenger door left open, waiting. Rhiannon barged past me, out through the kitchen, onto the balcony that ran alongside the front doors of the apartment block's second storey. She grabbed hold of the balustrade and looked down.

"We've talked about this Gordon," she shouted.

He looked up, grinned. "Doesn't matter," he said. "A bet is a bet."

"But you're my brother."

"Half brother."

"Oh really!!? Like that makes all the difference!"

Now this was shocking of course, but I could see immediately it let me off the hook. I mean a gentleman's wager was one thing, but the law was a contract that binds us all. I joined Rhiannon on the balcony.

"Bets off Gordon," I said. "She's staying with me."

Rhiannon looked at me relieved. Gordon however was furious. "You don't want to be breaking your word," he said. "Not to me. There'll be consequences."

"It doesn't matter. I can't allow this to happen."

Rhiannon linked her arm in mine and held on tightly. Gordon's face tightened, set itself into a grim warlike countenance. "You've just made a big mistake," he said. "A massive mistake actually, wait and see. I'm going to go and lay the table down in hell." And with that he got into the Peugeot, fired up the engine and screeched away.

I heard Rhiannon exhale and extricated my arm, turning to look at her. My face must have been asking a lot of questions because all she said was "I don't want to talk about it," then went back inside.

In the end we decided to put all these complications behind us and fix a date for the wedding. I think Rhiannon was especially looking forward to moving out of her flat and into the house. I booked a slot at the registry office, organised a reception at the Hen and everyone seemed pretty much happy with that. Most of all I was intrigued to meet

Rhiannon's parents. When the taxi arrived at my house, I was astounded to see Aaron step out of the cab, except that he was much older. In fact, he seemed to have aged shockingly in the past few months since I'd last encountered him, and it was disquietingly like looking at myself as a middle aged man. Seeing me at the door he grinned mischievously, obviously anticipating my surprise.

"Well boy, what did you think?" he asked.

"Think?" I responded, feeling confused.

"About Rhiannon." He started to take his luggage out of the back seat.

"She's your daughter?"

"Well yes, obviously," he said, putting down a suitcase on the pavement. "Fiona felt uncomfortable having her round the house, so this seemed the best place to send her, you being so chivalrous and all."

I had a multitude of questions whirling round my head. There was the time to account for of course, and looking at Aaron I could only conclude that it moved faster in some way where they were from. Then there was Gordon, but the first thing I asked was: "But don't you think it's odd, us looking so much like each other?"

"What's odd?" He looked at me sternly.

"Me and Rhiannon getting married."

"No, why?"

"Its just .. " I wasn't sure how to put it.

"There's one thing I need to ask you, Paul."

I shook myself out of my strange frame of mind, "..mm .. yes ..what's that?"

I watched him pay the taxi driver, who drove away, then he turned towards me and said: "Are you sure nothing happened with you and Fiona while you were over there?"

"Absolutely certain Aaron."

"Right, it's just .. I've never been sure .. it might have been while she was at her mothers maybe .."

We both stood there, me by the door and him on the pavement with the patio between us. " .. its the boys you see, Fiona just.."

I wasn't entirely sure what he meant. He brightened up suddenly. "Ah never mind," he said, "it's probably all nothing. Let's get this shebbang underway." He picked up his cases and we went inside.

The Changeling

The wedding went down a storm, and one of the best things about it for me was I met Rhiannon's other brother Gideon, who had just moved up this way. He was Gordon's twin but a totally different kettle of fish I have to say, really top bloke. He apologised for his brother's behaviour and offered to take me out fishing as a way of making up for it all. We spent many pleasant afternoons by the canal, but eventually of course I had other commitments and our sojourns had to be put on hold. Rhiannon gave birth to little baby Dylan and any spare time I had, when I wasn't working, was spent minding the child and giving Rhiannon the chance to rest. Gideon understood though. Like I said, top bloke.

One of the things I haven't mentioned is the wedding present he brought. This was an heirloom from his mother's side of the family and an attempt on his part to build bridges between Rhiannon and Fiona, who were still incommunicado. It was an antique bronze cooking pot, more of a cauldron when I think about it, and had been in the family's possession for countless generations. It also came with a big ol' mixing stick for stirring the cauldron, and I was told by Aaron that this would be my responsibility. Having grown used to microwaves and ovens though, I have to admit, we had some trouble using it, and our soups and stews tended to turn out rather watery. The hobs just weren't big enough and I had some idea of building a cooking pit once we moved to a bigger place.

It was sometime later, I started to have my suspicions about Dylan. By the age of six months, he had grown to the size of a two year old and was walking and tottering about and starting to put sentences together. Also, he was a bit scaly. It was the kind of mystical jiggery pokery I'd come to expect from Rhiannon's side of the family.

These suspicions were rather sheepishly confirmed to me by Gideon one day as we were sat by the canal again, waiting for a catch. The day was downcast, grey with a light drizzle and the fish were failing to bite. Instead, we watched the rain ripple on the water's surface. He told me that he had been encouraged in establishing this friendship by Gordon, naively believing it was an honest attempt to make reparations for his boorish behaviour, but more recent conversations, more specifically Gordon's interest in knowing the dates and times of our fishing soirees had led him to believe his brother still harboured dishonourable intentions.

So, the next time me and Gideon were due to meet, I packed my fishing tackle as normal and left the house, but instead of heading for the canal, I went into a bus shelter at the end of the road, took off my fishing jacket and hat and replaced them with an anonymous kagoul and observed the house. Forty five minutes later Gordon turned up in the Peugeot. I was fuming, of course. I stormed out of the shelter leaving all my gear behind me and made my way to the back of the house where my van was parked. I unlocked the back of it and took out a hatchet, then went into the building.

I found them together in the front room. Gordon was sat on the sofa and Rhiannon was on an armchair looking apprehensive. Dylan was running around in a nappy, tottering on his little legs, as Gordon threw him mice, which the boy attempted to catch and eat. Just as I walked in he got one by the tail and giggling with delight, put it in his mouth and chomped on it and I heard the bones crunch and the mouse squeak for a while as he sucked down the guts, the tail wiggling, and then he spat this out along with the bones and fur. He was drooling a bit of blood which Rhiannon mopped up with a babywipe.

"So, what the hell is going on here?" I demanded.

"Paul," laughed Gordon. He seemed very pleased to see me. "I was wondering if you'd ever turn up. Take a pew, why don't you?"

"Not until I get some answers, no," I said, brandishing the axe in what I hoped was a menacing manner.

"It's not what you think," Rhiannon sighed. "Gordon just gave us this child to foster, while our own is being fostered elsewhere. It's part of a deal I made."

"A deal? What sort of deal?"

"That Gordon leave you alone. We made the switch the week after I gave birth, when you 'popped out' to help Gideon fix his bike." I noticed a faint trace of accusation there. However, it was the idea I needed 'protection' from Gordon that really made me angry, so I ran forward and butted him with the haft of the hatchet and then gave him a really good kicking. It was pretty bloody and the sofa was ruined. Soon he was pleading with me to stop and swore never to come round this way again. I remembered what he said about his people meaning what they say, or was it saying what they mean. I guess it amounted to the same thing. So, I let him make his exit, staggering with his shattered face out of the front door, and stood at the window until I saw that damn Peaugot drive away.

"That's the way to deal with things," I told Rhiannon.

She seemed upset though, it was still her brother after all. "It was the kind of situation I was hoping to avoid," she said. "What if he takes it out on the real Dylan?"

"He wouldn't do that would he?"

"It's difficult to say."

"We need to find the boy then."

"And what about ..." she nodded towards our foster child, who had been sitting watching the unfolding events with a playful curiosity and now was wandering around the room hoping to find more mice. I noticed he was starting to grow fins. I was still holding the hatchet. I put it down next to the sofa.

"Let's talk about it over dinner," I said.

"Mmm, that was lovely," said Gideon. "You're getting the hang of that old cooking pot after all."

"The secret is in making the correct stock," Rhiannon replied modestly.

"And your young ward?"

"He had to go," I interrupted quickly. "Just the problems of getting him into a good school."

"I understand. Which brings us to the actual Dylan, have you been having any dreams which might help us to locate him, I wonder?"

"Actually yes," said Rhiannon. "I have this dream where he's in a stable and this monstrous claw reaches in and tries to find him but keeps grabbing the newborn colts instead, but now the colts are all taken and I know he's going to be next."

"Mm, well that's a start I suppose, nothing more specific?"

"Just that he has yellow hair."

"Ah okay, we'll start with the nearest stables and then circle I suppose, though I'm worried it might take some time."

So was I, but we organised for Rhiannon to take on some work while I was away, seamstress work doing alterations and a couple of cleaning jobs. She didn't seem happy about this but it was necessary. Me and Gideon set off on our mission the next day. I remember it being cold and damp with a light mist, the kind that dissolves the edges of the landscape. I drove the van out of town until we reached the ringroad and then took the left fork, which headed outwards through some drab fields and bare trees. As I drove on, we faded in the mist disappearing into our surroundings.

Cinders

Luke, as he was known, was easily distinguished from his three foster brothers by his blonde hair, while they were all in possession of dark, tangled mops. The whole family were a bunch of notorious ne'er do wells, who owned a stable and were well connected with the racing world, but were also known to dabble in the odd burglary or two. Lovable scamps.

One day, they were out on their trials bikes, hunting down rabbits and pheasants with the help of their bull terrier Fritzi. The morning had been somewhat successful, and they were returning to their parked 4 by 4 dragging their mangled culls behind them and trying to avoid the attentions of the local Wildlife Police. Fergal was the eldest brother, and his bike was ahead of the pack when he signalled them to slow down by raising his hand and then brought his bike to a halt. Luke pulled up alongside him.

"What is it?" he asked. The other two brothers, Farley and Fraser came to a stop on either side of them, while a slavering Fritzi brought up the rear.

Fergal pointed in the direction of the 4 by 4. There was a man leaning against the rear of it. Luke squinted his eyes.

"That looks like my godfather Gideon," he said.

"Are you certain?" Fergal asked.

"Yes," said Luke, so the foursome started up their bikes again and rode forward until they were next to the vehicle. Luke dismounted first and went to shake his hand.

"Godfather," he asked, "What are you doing here?"

"Looking for a favour," said Gideon. "Donald told me I might find you this way."

"What sort of favour?" They had been joined by the three brothers, who shook Gideon's hand also.

"The man who smashed my brother's face and took his eye out, he's round here somewhere. I want him taking care of."

The four siblings looked at each other.

"And what's he doing round here?" asked Fergal.

"I brought him, didn't I? Messed with the fuel tank before we set off and now the cunt is stranded. Told him I was going to look for a garage."

"Right," said Fergal, "and Don knows about this?"

"Of course he does. And then when it's done, I need a word with Luke."

"Oh, what about?" Luke replied.

"Your mother's been asking about you. It might be time you got reacquainted."

Luke froze and felt the ground shift under his feet for a second. "Really," he asked, his voice sounding strange to himself, "are you sure?"

"A long time ago she asked me to bring you here, for your own safety, but now you are fully grown. It is time."

Luke hesitated. It had indeed been a long time, from when he was a babe and life with the McGintys was all he had ever known. He wiped a tear from his eye.

Fergal was looking at Luke intently. He could see how much it meant to him. "A favour for a favour, is that right?" he asked Gideon.

"That's right," the man replied.

"Okay," said Fergal, "we're in."

They pulled up in the four by four across the road from where I'd parked the van. Gideon got out accompanied by two men I took to be mechanics, so I opened my door and went out to meet them. The blonde one was carrying a holdall and as soon as they saw me, he reached in and pulled out a sawn off shotgun. I looked at Gideon to see if there was some kind of mistake, and then the man pointed it and pulled the trigger and there was a bang and a cloud of smoke and the blast tore open a big hole in my belly and flung me back against the van. I slid down the side of it leaving a bloody trail and I could look down and see my guts. The man put down the holdall, and the dark haired man reached in and pulled out a long bladed knife and a hacksaw. I had a bad feeling about it all.

"No, Luke really," I was saying. "I am your father."

I wasn't sure what they'd done with the rest of the body, but my dismembered head was in a sports bag in the back of the four by four and Luke was driving it back towards my house. The purpose was unclear.

"I wish you'd stop saying that," he replied.

I was quite surprised - what with my head being hacked off - at being able to speak at all, but then again, the unreal had become par for the course lately, so I went along with it. "I can't help it being true, can I?" There was no reply from the front seat.

"So, what's the purpose of all this, have they told you?"

"They wanted rid of you, and wanted me to be the one to do it."

"So you could meet your mother?"

"Yes."

"Excited about it?"

"Yes."

"Well, that's something I suppose."

But when we got back there, we found the house empty. Luke used my keys to unlock the door and then placed the bag containing my head on the kitchen table. I heard him moving around.

"There's no one here," I heard him say eventually.

"Maybe she's at work," I said helpfully.

"Where's that?"

"Different places, cleaning .. just a temporary arrangement while I was away."

"Is this her?"

"Well, I can't see, can I?"

He took me out of the bag and propped me up against the toaster, then showed me a framed photograph he'd taken down from the wall - Rhiannon in her lace wedding dress and me next to her in a tuxedo. I blinked my eyelids apart and said, "Yes, of course".

"She looks angelic."

"She tended to do that, yes."

"And you really must be my father then."

"I said so, didn't I?"

"Hmm." He put the photo down and paced the room a bit. "I wonder why they didn't say. Maybe thought I wouldn't go through with it if I knew."

"What did they say?"

"That I was to hand the head over to Gordon and the rest would be explained."

"What about the rest of me?"

"Stored in a freezer, until we can decide what to do with it."

"Oh, nice."

There was a silence. His attention had been drawn by a post it note, stuck to the side of the fridge. "Red Lodge, 6am. What's that?"

I thought about it, creasing my brow. "Hotel and conference centre," I remembered, "Outskirts of town. Sometimes."

"Sometimes. What does that mean?"

"Sometimes it's there and sometimes it's not." I frowned. This had never struck me as strange before but now it did.

He looked at me. "You know, they told me I'd been fostered because my father was delusional. That he was a danger to his children, that one had already disappeared."

I mulled this over, that way you do when something doesn't taste right in your mouth. "I wish this was a delusion, right now," I said, "it might come as a relief, actually."

He stared at me for a while, then nodded and gazed back around the kitchen. "Yeah," he said, "I know what you mean."

By the evening, Rhiannon hadn't returned so Luke put me back in the sports bag and we drove off to the Red Lodge. It was a glass squarish construction surrounded by a big tarmac carpark. Modern architecture really likes to congratulate itself on discovering the square. Well done, modern architecture I say, your creativity and sense of decoration astounds me. Anyway, as you drove in - if I remember - there was a sign, a large oval supported by two posts bearing the hotel's logo - a green branch sprouting red flowers. We came to a halt and I heard the rear door open and I was picked up and slung over Luke's shoulder and we went inside. I heard him ask about Rhiannon on the reception desk and then we were sat down waiting for a while.

Eventually the bag unzipped and Luke was looking in at me.

"This is ridiculous," he said, "the reception guy has disappeared and this lobby is deserted."

"What did he say?"

"She wasn't one of the guests and then I suggested she might be working here and he said he'd have to go and check. That was twenty minutes ago."

"Let's go look around."

He nodded, and I was picked up again. There was a feeling of absence in the hotel lobby, like it was just there waiting for people. Outside in the dark there was nothing except the lights hanging over the carpark and rain had started to patter against the glass.

We went round the ground floor first, into the conference hall. It was obvious some kind of event had been going on. The lights were on and seats were clustered before the podium, with discarded pamphlets lying on top of some of them. Luke picked one up - 'Red Branch Training' he read, obviously something in house. Inside was a lot of blurb about being inspiring as a leader - 'a new dawn for the service industry, learning the acronyms,' he murmured out loud, before our brains sort of switched off, the way anyone normals does when confronted with that kind of material. Still, if this had been a conference, where were the guests? The adjoining bar was empty too, although it had been occupied: there were glasses on tables, some still containing dregs, empty packets of peanuts, crumbs. It was late mind you, maybe people were just tucked up in bed and they hadn't got round to clearing up. The absence of staff was weird though, it didn't feel right.

Luke went back to reception and nosied around behind the desk. He moved the mouse on one of the computers and the screen flickered on, showing a grid of cctv images. No one outside, just rain lashing over the floodlit tarmac, we could hear it .. Some of them showed the corridors on each floor.

"There she is," he said.

"Let me see!" It was frustrating, being in the bag. He unzipped it and tilted it up so I was facing the screen. The camera showed the corridor from above, at sort of a distorted angle. She was on the seventh floor, in a plain housekeeping uniform, a sort of ugly violet tabard, pushing her cleaner's trolley, her hair tied back. We saw her knock on the door to one of the rooms then go in.

"Do you see anybody else?" he asked.

My eyes scanned the grid of images. "There," I said, "top left." There was a man leaving one of the rooms. He was wearing a suit and one of those eyemasks, the type you'd wear to a masked ball, if that was your thing. He looked each way, then went down the corridor and got into the elevator.

"Right," said Luke with a sort of tight determination, then I was zipped up and picked up again and we were heading for the stairs. He took them two or three at a time, jostling me about in the bag and reached the seventh floor not much out of breath. He kept himself fit obviously. We went up to the room with the cleaning cart outside and swung the door open.

"What the hell," I heard him mutter. I was put down.

"What's happening?" I asked.

"There's no one here," he said, exasperated. Then, "Wait."

"What is it?"

"A plimsole on the floor. The kind cleaners wear."

"Just the one?"

"Just the one, yes."

"Wait a second," I remembered I'd had some special plimsolls made for her, with a custom insole, so her feet wouldn't ache so much. I asked Luke to check.

"It has the insole, yes," he said.

Then I found myself thinking about the man we'd seen upstairs. I had an uncomfortable feeling, I don't know why. "We need to check the elevator as well," I said.

Luke must have been thinking along the same lines, because he just leant down to pick up the shoe, which he stuffed in his pocket and then picked me up and took me back into the corridor. "First floor," he said, "going down." Then we were running and took the stairs downwards, three at a time again and it was even bumpier. I was rolling around in that bag like a loose cabbage. We ran straight for a bit then came to an abrupt halt. I was facing sideways pressed against the rubber and feeling horribly dizzy. We still weren't moving but I could hear chatter, liveliness. It seemed brighter. We moved backwards a bit and the bag zipped open once more.

"What is it?" I asked quietly, out of the side of my mouth.

"I don't know pops," said Luke, "but I reckon we're not in Kansas anymore." He gave me a quick glimpse. We were back in the lobby, but now it was occupied and bright sunlight was streaming in through the glass. Outside the car park across the way was different, smaller and full now of vehicles, and beyond this were some fields and hills that I didn't recognise. The conference centre had moved again, but now maybe there was the chance to find out where to.

"Stay quiet," he said, and shuttered me up again. We moved through the people back to reception. As I found out later, it was a different receptionist from the one Luke had spoken to earlier, shorter and with a Welsh accent. Next to the doors leading to the conference room, a board has been put up: 'Annual Red Branch Masked Ball - this way.'

" ... private party .." I heard. " ... can't let you in I'm afraid .."

mumble, mumble, some argument ...

" .. could ask her to step out ... identify her ..."

We were moving around to the other side of the desk. Luke with the receptionist was checking out the cameras, of which there were two in the conference hall. A seemingly impossible task to identify Rhiannon of course, with there being so many people and all of them wearing masks. The podium apparently had been cleared to make space for a chamber quintet and there was some dancing and a lot of hobnobbing at the bar and the buffet tables set up around the edge.

Luke frowned and peered closer, trying to make out individual figures among the indistinct pixelated throng. The receptionist was stood to one side, looking at him as you might a performing dog to see if he had mastered a new trick.

There were many women with blonde hair, but his attention was drawn to one who was dancing with a tuxedo'd man, hobbling slightly and not so much being led as pulled around the improvised dance space. She was wearing a simple white dress and a mask made of lace and filigree.

" zoom ... move the camera down .." I heard, and unless you're slow on the uptake, you won't be surprised to hear she was wearing an anachronistic singular plimsole.

" ... talk to her please .." said Luke in a self congratulatory tone.

"Of course, sir," said the receptionist politely, although you got the sense he was resisting the impulse to pat Luke on the head. He ducked into the conference hall and returned with Rhiannon five minutes later and brought her over to reception. She had removed her mask, which she now held in her hand and walked slightly awkwardly in her one shoe.

"Yes?" she enquired.

Luke grinned goofily, I guess it was an awkward thing to come right out and say. "I'm Luke," he began. "Paul came to find me, I think you're my mother .." It was as good an opener as possible I suppose.

"Oh," she responded, a coolness in her voice. "Really?"

Now, I suppose in a naive way I'd expected her to instinctively recognise her child and much emotion and embracing to ensue, so this was kind of anticlimactic.

"Yes, I can prove it. I have papers. Also, I have your special plimsole." Strangely, this last seemed to settle matters more than the mention of official documentation.

" .. well, I suppose you must be then," she said. "Where's Paul?"

"Ahh..."

Yes, I could tell this was going to be a very awkward reunion.

Flowerface

The conference centre as it happened, had moved not too far from where Rhiannon grew up: in the house where I'd met Fiona round about two years ago. I was keen to see how the garden was looking, now it had had the chance to get established a bit, so we all took a drive down there in the van, Rhiannon phoning ahead.

Luke seemed somewhat troubled as he drove through the Welsh countryside, and it wasn't difficult to guess what was bothering him.

"So, if you're my mum, how come you're so young?" he asked eventually. And she was still young and attractive.

"It must have been where Gideon had you fostered," Rhiannon replied, "probably with some of the faerie folk. Time moves differently there."

Luke thought about this and it made sense. There had been all those pagan rituals.

"And my real name is Dylan?"

"Yes."

"Hmm." He frowned. I guess it was a lot to get used to all at once. "And the real Luke," he asked. "What happened to him?"

Rhiannon kept her gaze firmly fixed on the passing landscape.

"He's somewhere safe," I said, "don't worry."

Even though I was aware myself of the time thing, it was still a shock for me when I arrived back at the house. The garden was not just established, it was verdant, with the small shrubs I'd planted now fully grown, the rockery all mossy and the apple tree I'd planted no longer a sapling but a good size tree all laden with blossom. Then there were Aaron and Fiona, no longer young but a retired couple in their sixties.

Well, the introductions were made and everyone tried to be cordial, but to my eyes it was clear that Fiona still harboured obscure feelings of jealousy and resentment towards her daughter, more so when she saw how little she had aged. Aaron though, was his usual amenable self. A party was made in the garden, and if I say so myself, it really was a delightful spot. The clematis and jasmine I'd planted at the edge of the patio now ran up the side of the house, and there were potted lavender and rosemary and fuschias, and pink daisies running between the flags, and then a rose garden next to the rockery with its alpines and succulents, and then laurels and geraniums and snapdragons in the borders. The flowers all gave off their scents, from the fresh citrus tang of the wallflowers to the ineffable perfumes of the roses to the murky undercurrent of the herbs, and best of all, birds seemed drawn to the tree and serenaded us all the time with song.

Then the white painted wrought iron furniture was arranged on the patio and I was given a very convenient spot atop the table and there were egg and cress sandwiches and a spot of cider.

"So, Dylan," Aaron said, "we need to discuss the matter of your inheritance."

"Inheritance?" Dylan said. "Oh no, I wasn't expecting anything like that. I'm just happy to be reunited with my family." He looked at his mother hopefully and tenderly. It was uncomfortable, given the nearness of their ages and Fiona picked up on this too.

"All the same, me and Fiona aren't going to be around forever," carried on Aaron obliviously, "and we have this lovely house that's going to need looking after and then also, we have a sizable amount saved up. Is it something you'd be interested in?"

"Well, I guess. I just don't want to let anyone down."

"Oh, I'm sure you won't. It's just the inheritance comes with conditions."

"Conditions? What kind of conditions?"

"Rather arcane ones I'm afraid, that come down from a more medieval age. No doubt now they seem silly."

We waited.

"First that you must never approach the town of Wrexham in a counter clockwise manner."

We all laughed, which broke the tension.

"Sure," said Dylan sheepishly, "I reckon I can do that."

"Good. And then second that you must never follow three reds to a red house."

"I'm sorry?" We laughed again.

"I know," said Aaron, "they don't quite make sense. My understanding is that they relate to some sort of old feud - a Campbell/Glencoe kind of thing."

"Well, I guess I can manage that too," said Dylan. I was sort of proud of him.

"And then third that you must never give shelter to a woman wearing a black veil."

"Sure, why not," Dylan said with a grin. "In for a penny, in for a pound."

"I want to add a condition of my own," said Rhiannon. We all looked at her. Well, I turned my eyes as best I could.

"Really darling," said Aaron, "what would that be?"

"That he never wed mortal woman."

There was a silence. We were all a bit shocked.

"Really petal," said Aaron eventually. "Why would you stymie the lad in such a way. Besides, an inheritance is based on the idea of heredity, on there being legitimate descendants, it's implicit in the word."

"There lies your contradiction."

Aaron looked at his daughter disapprovingly. "I can see you're in a contrary mood yourself," he said.

 "All the same, there it is."

"What you're saying is, we find him a faerie wife. You know that will be trouble, don't you?"

"I don't know, Paul," - she turned to address me - "would you say that I'd been a lot of trouble?"

"Well .... " I thought that my current predicament spoke for itself.

"And how would you feel about that Dylan?" Aaron asked, "A faerie wife."

"That sounds alright, yeah," he said, although I imagined he looked with strange regret at his mother.

"Can that be organised, Fiona?" Aaron looked at his wife. She was watching Rhiannon and smiling strangely. After a while she nodded.

"I expect so. I'll talk to the boys, see if they know if anyone's available."

And I was about to express my own opinions, about Gordon and Gideon's fundamental lack of trustworthiness, when Fiona reached across for the jug of cider, ostensibly to make a toast, and 'accidentally' knocked me from the table.

"Oh dear," she said, "how clumsy of me," as I rolled across the lawn. She got up from her chair and scooted over to pick me up by my lank hair. "Bits of grass all over you," she added. "I'll just take you inside and wipe you down with a damp cloth."

I was a bit stunned by the fall and in the kitchen really before I knew it. By that time, she had placed me on the counter, wiped the grass very roughly off my face with aforesaid cloth, and then crouched herself down to look me right in the eyes. Her stare was very hard, like pieces of flint.

"Paul," she said. "You need to think a moment before you starting saying bad things about our boys, or honest to god, I am going to fucking microwave you, do we have that straight?"

"Marry your nephew?" Blodwyn said to Gordon. They were in a motel room, an inexpensive place just off the highway. "Isn't it bad enough you make me dress up as your sister?" She looked at herself in the mirror, in the silver blonde wig and the floral dress.

"You're being paid for it aren't you, you scrubber?" said Gordon. He was sat up naked in bed and scratching his good eye. "You're not being paid to be fucking particular."

"Not enough to get married either," she retorted. "That goes way beyond the call of duty."

"Not even when there's a big inheritance involved?"

"Ahhh ... "

"Have your attention now do I?" he sneered.

"Maybe."

"Maybe .. goddamn absolutely I do."

"Farley won't like it."

"Well, he shouldn't have fallen in love with a whore then, should he?"

"He's young, earnest."

"Yeah, we were all that once. Big Don's given it the go ahead anyway. He'll straighten it with the lad."

"I see." Blodwyn took the money off the dresser and put it in her handbag. "So, this inheritance, how do you plan to get your share, once I'm married?"

"You let us worry about that darling. You just play your part. That look though, you need to make it permanent, get your hair cropped and dyed. There's a couple of other details too."

He smiled happily. He felt the deal was done. Blodwyn took her handbag and left the room, went down the corridor and stairs and exited the motel through the lobby. She took out her phone to call a cab and looked out over the car park. Above the conifers at one end, she could see the moon. It was bright and swollen.

We spent several weeks at the house. It was a happy time. The weather was good and there were parties in the garden where me, Aaron and Rhiannon told jokes and the tree was always full of singing birds and good food came out of the kitchen. Dylan and his mother went for walks in the countryside and seemed to be reconciled somewhat. Even Fiona put aside her differences and came with us some evenings to the village pub - The White Stag - where with my head propped up on the bar, I would sip ale through a straw and swap tall tales and stories with the locals. As promised, I kept my mouth shut about Gordon and Gideon, even when they turned up and joined in with our parties. I couldn't help but notice though, one night they and Dylan were huddled in a snug in the corner, whispering and looking at me as I traded yarns at the bar.*

The next day they packed me up in a carrier bag and put me in the back of the 4 by 4 again and we drove out until we reached the border, then they pulled the vehicle up to the verge and Gordon picked me up again while Gideon opened up the boot and took out a spade. It was cloudy, the weather was starting to turn.

I sighed. "What's happening now?" I asked.

Gordon looked into the bag. "We've explained things to Dylan," he said, "and this is where we leave you." He grinned suddenly. "What if I were to tell you Paul, that we never did swap children, that the original Dylan was yours all along? Not even my mother figured that one out."

"No," I said. "No, that couldn't be."

I could hear the sound of digging nearby.

"Well, maybe it is. In which case tis my child inherits everything. You need to think about that, while you're buried beneath the sod and the worms nibble at your eyeballs."

Then unceremoniously, they rolled my head out of the bag so I fell into the hole they'd just dug, about three feet down and they covered me over with soil and it became very dark. Somewhere up above I heard the faint sound of an engine receding into the distance, and still nowadays I hear the sound of passing traffic, and occasionally someone stops and I hear their low murmured talk but then they just drive away again. That is how it was for many years.

They dropped Dylan off back at the house, the one with the door knocker in the shape of the green man. It was his now of course. His mother had stayed behind in Wales and the only member of the family he saw was his apparent father Gordon, who he tried to like but couldn't, although he kept his secret misgivings hidden. The only thing to look forward to was the forthcoming marriage. He was delighted when his father brought forth Blodwyn, with her fair hair and her face like blossom. So, he waited patiently. He missed his brothers, and the life he was making, for now he used my van to earn a crust of his own - tarmacing driveways - often seemed arduous and dull. The weather didn't help, it was cold and misty and there had been no sunny days since he left the garden and the only scent was that of boiling bitumen.

"I don't like your hair like that," said Farley. "I like it when it was red and fell to your shoulders." They were in the caravan he was occupying on the fields next to some stables, near to a patch of woodland.

"It was necessary for the marriage," explained Blodwyn.

"I like that even less. The man who touches you I should kill him."

She laughed. "A lot of men have touched me," she said, "you know that already."

"But not as a wife. That is what I wanted for myself."

"When I get the money. After that you might kill him."

"That is why, you won't tell me who he is."

"In case your passions get the better of you afore then."

"Do you blame me? You inspire passion Blodwyn. There is not a man I wouldn't kill for you."

"Your brother even?"

"Then I would kill you both." She looked at him. It was the most exciting thing she knew, to drive such energies. He was looking back at her with dark abject hunger. She let him tear her clothes and push her onto his makeshift bed.

She left several hours later as dawn was breaking, in a borrowed tshirt and tracksuit bottoms, getting into a taxi and heading back to her flat. Some distance away - the Peaguot parked up in a quiet shady lane - Gordon watched her through his one good eye. Dylan was in the back seat.

"You understand?" he said to the young man. "With a faerie wife, it's never going to be straightforward. She expects you to get rid of rivals, to some extent."

Dylan had been watching Blodwyn exit the caravan and cross the bare compacted dirt surrounding it until she reached the cab. Her cropped blonde hair was caught by the breeze as she opened the door and got inside. It was hard to explain what he felt. Not quite jealousy, but something more like distaste. Most of all he hated the man in the front seat for bringing him here and showing him this, but then again hate, his upbringing had taught him, was something that was easily transferred.

"Who is in there?" he asked. "

A fortune hunter," said Gordon. "They plot for your inheritance no doubt. You have to prove to her that you're worth it. Obviously, she suspects a weakness."

"I understand," Dylan said. He picked up the sawn off shotgun from the floor of the car. "Let's go," he said. Gordon started the car and drove until they were on a stretch of road near to the woods next to the caravan. Dylan got out of the car carrying the gun, and hoisted himself over a wall so that he was in the woods and scurried through the trees and patches of morning mist until he could see the caravan. Keeping low he carefully circled around until he could see through one of its windows: a figure moving about in there through the net curtain. He got closer and pointed the gun at the patch of wall where the figure must be standing and fired it - BANG BANG BANG - leaving jagged holes in the wall, then ran back through the trees and mist to where Gordon was revving the Peugeot, leapt the wall and they drove off.

Don opened the door of the caravan and went inside followed by his wife Maude. In the small carpeted living area he could see the shredded remains of his son, in a sticky pool of blood, with streaks of matter spread over the surrounding walls and furniture. There were three gunshot punctures in the metal wall facing out to the woods. They looked at the boy grimly, blankly. Fergal and Fraser came in next. Fergal went pale.

"Who would dare do this?" he whispered.

"I don't know but they'll pay," said Don. "Isn't that right my love?" He turned to look at Maude. She was a stout imposing woman, more formidable than Don himself.

"They better pay," she uttered in a thin voice. "All here will swear it to me. Whosoever did this, none here will rest until they bring terrible retribution upon them."

Don looked at the boys. "We swear it Ma," said Fergal, "of course we do."

"Swear it on the soul of your mother when she dies."

They hesitated.

"DO IT!" she screeched.

"We swear for the sake of your dead soul Ma. That it goes to hell if we fail." All made the same terrible promise, even Don.

"And if I go there, I'll be waiting for the alls of yer," she said. "I make that my promise to you."

Don gave out a grunt of assent and looked round the room again. He noticed the state of the bed and then the torn dress that was scrunched up at the bottom. He went for a closer look and examined the pillow, and then lifted off a white-blonde hair, red at the root.

"Ah," he said, "I think I understand what might have happened here."

"You're going to need to hide out for a while," said Gordon. "There's people will be looking for you."

"Who?" asked Dylan. They were driving out of the countryside, onto a main road leading to the highway.

"Friends of the departed of course. I've no doubt he's been waxing bitter about your engagement and they'll be wanting to talk to you."

"I didn't do this to spend my time in hiding."

"Of course not. It's just a matter of lying low until tempers cool down. Then I'll go talk to them."

Dylan chewed over the matter, watching the landscape slide past as he did so. "Where?" he said eventually.

"We're nearly there," said Gordon. There were roadworks up ahead. "It looks as though I'll have to make a diversion though." He took a sliproad that brought them onto a ringroad, which he followed round counter clockwise then turned off so that they passed by a sign indicating they were heading for Wrexham.

Dylan frowned as he looked at the sign. Then he realised what had happened. He started to say something, but ... what? It was just an unfortunate coincidence that's all, and the other two conditions of the contract were so ridiculous he couldn't imagine ever breaking them. Gordon must have done it by accident. That's all it was.

Red Lodge

Dylan spent three days sequestered in the Holiday Inn in Wrexham before getting the call from Gordon: that Blodwyn was ready to meet him at the Red Lodge conference centre, the one where he'd first met his mother. As for the friction the assassination of her lover had caused: not to worry, Gordon felt it could be smoothed out with a small portion of the impending inheritance.

So, Dylan drove out to the Lodge in a hired car. He was some way there when a builder's van overtook him on the left hand side and moved into his lane, so that he had to slow down. To his irritation, just as he was about to take the turning for the Lodge, the van turned off too, and every time he thought about overtaking, the van seemed to anticipate this and speed up in turn. Then they reached the Red Lodge and the van pulled into the car park, so he was made to follow there also, and when it came to a halt and the driver got out, Dylan saw that he had red hair, as did his two passengers who disembarked on the other side. So it seemed he had broken the second clause of the contract. A dark chill went through him. He heard a fluttering of wings and a cawing, and saw that a crow had flown down to land on the Lodge's oval sign nearby. He laughed nervously to himself. 'Good job I'm not superstitious' he thought, and the third clause was yet to be broken. A woman with a black veil. Well, he wouldn't invite any woman inside, not without seeing her first. And what were the chances of him breaking that before the marriage could take place? Very slim. The crow watched him as he walked from the car over to the Lodge's entrance.

Gordon and the gorgeous Blodwyn were waiting in the lobby. As soon as he saw her, Dylan thought that all the recent complications were entirely justified. What's more, Gordon brought a message from Fiona, that a register had been appointed and that the marriage could take place at a chapel in the Lodge itself. It looked like everything was going to be wrapped up soon.

In the Lodge's restaurant, the red haired builder, a man called Cullen, looked through one of its glass walls into the lobby and observed Dylan and Blodwyn as they headed for the lifts. His two brothers sat opposite him, eating their bacon and egg sandwiches. He took out his phone and keyed in a number.

"They're here," he said.

Dylan and Blodwyn had rooms next to each other. He was in a state of great anticipation and very much looking forward to the wedding night. So, that by the time the receptionist phoned the room and told him that Fiona was waiting downstairs, he had quite forgot himself and told him to send her up. He was wondering about the ceremony and how the invitations were going to be sent out - particularly to his mother and his foster family, who he was looking forward to seeing again - when the knock came at the door. "Come in," he called, and Fiona entered the room and to his disbelief was wearing a black veil. At that moment, the crow he'd seen earlier landed on the windowsill outside his room and cawed. He stepped back in horror as Fiona drew aside the veil and he saw that she had aged another ten years and that now her bitterness had rendered her crone like. She had overdone her make up so that her face was plastered white and contrasted terribly with her bright red lipstick.

"Fiona, why are you dressed in black?" he asked, stuttering.

"Aaron is dead," she said, "but then you wouldn't have heard, would you, gallivanting all over the place.... "

"No, I didn't hear."

"And I'm aware also, that you've broken all the clauses. That means the weddings off, of course, and the inheritance too." She shook her head. "Now it all goes to my boys, as it should in the first place. Aaron always had this notion, that they weren't his, you see."

"Gordon and Gideon, they're what, my step brothers?"

"It's com...." Then the telephone rang again. Dylan looked at it and Fiona just waited in silence as it continued to ring. With a feeling of stealthily approaching doom, he picked it up. It was Fergal.

"Luke," the man said. "Why did you do it? Kill Farley."

"Farley?" he tried to think. "Hold on, that was Farley?"

"You didn't know?"

"In all honesty I didn't."

"Ah." There was a silence.

"That puts me in a bind then," Fergal continued. "You understand we can't let it go, this being family."

"I understand. But listen it was G....."

The line went dead suddenly. He looked over to see that Fiona had pulled the cord from its socket.

"No no no," she said. "It's all over, the best you can do is accept it." Luke rushed out into the corridor and opened the door to Blodwyn's room. It was empty. Then back in the corridor he saw that someone was coming up in the lift so he made for the stairwell. He was halfway down, turning a corner when he saw Fraser coming up towards him with a knife. He switched direction and ran up to the previous level and burst out on to the third floor landing. He got halfway down the corridor when Big Don came around the corner with a shotgun. He faltered to an abrupt halt. Fraser was behind him. He took in a few ragged breaths.

"Listen," he said, "It was Gordon and Gideon .. "

"Now now," said Don. "I thought I brought you up not to tell tales." He was levelling the shotgun when the lift pinged open to Luke's left. He threw himself inside as the shotgun erupted - blowing Fraser's brains over the corridor walls - knocking down Fergal who was inside and in desperation pressing the ground floor button. They descended locked in together.

Fergal looked at him with tears in his eyes. They were both crouched on the floor of the lift.

"Why Luke?" he asked. "Didn't I treat you as a brother? I loved you even more than my brothers. Why?"

"I was tricked."

Fergal nodded. It made sense.

"We've all been tricked I think," he said. "Don isn't even my father you know. I think Gideon is. That's why he brought you to be raised with me."

"So what are we fighting for?"

"I've sworn it, I have no choice."

Luke looked at him. He saw that it was true. "Do you remember," he said, "when we were twelve and that farmer caught us trying to steal his quad bike ..."

"and we ran and I got caught on that barbed wire."

"I cut you loose just in time."

"Yes," Fergal laughed. The lift was still going down. It seemed to be taking an abnormally long time.

"When we were younger we built that bike track, must have spent every day down there. You teaching me to trap hares."

"You built that raft remember, and we'd go jumping off the waterfall. Steal sweets from the other kids as they came home from school."

"We never went."

"Hardly ever."

"They were fine days."

"Yes, they were." Then Fergal tried to get the knife from his pocket and Luke lunged at him and got him by the throat and throttled him, banging his head against the wall of the lift as Fergal jammed the knife into his side, and Luke let go one hand and grabbed Fergals wrist as the mans other hand wrapped around his own throat, and then he let go and punched Fergal hard in the nose, breaking and splattering it and the man's grip loosened so Luke got hold of the knife, pulled it out of his side and forced it into Fergal's throat so that it sliced the larynx. Fergal spasmed and gurgled and then was still. The lift came to a halt and the doors opened.

Luke looked out into the lobby. It was eerily empty again. Outside storm clouds had gathered and rain was pouring down upon the carpark, bouncing off the tarmac. The only vehicle he could see out there was his own, apart from that it was deserted. Even the builder's van had gone. He looked at the grotesque sight of his dead brother pinned against the side of the lift and staggered mournfully into the reception area. There were three crows waiting on the sign out there now. He ran out into the rain and got in his car.

"I don't know what to do," said Luke. He was sat on the damp grass of the verge where the twins had buried me with the car parked up nearby. Up above my skull, a young hawthorn had started to grow, full of white blossom, and I found it was this that was easiest to talk through.

"Gone back to see your mother?"

"I've tried but I can't find the house. Fiona seems to have moved it somehow." He looked at his side where the wound had been stitched at the hospital. The tshirt he was wearing was stained with a great blotch of dried blood and he felt very weak. He was meant to be resting.

"Hmmm." I mulled it over. "You know it's been pretty boring down here the last ten years."

"Yeah look, I'm really sorry about that. Well, about everything to be honest."

"Never mind. There's one thing .. once you've been down here a while, the grubs tend to get a bit chatty, when they're not munching on you that is. And now with the tree, birds come down and they tell me things too .. secrets."

"That sounds alright, at least you don't get the crows." He looked around. There were six of them now, perched on a telegraph wire, watching him. "What kind of secrets anyway?"

"This is where you need to listen."

Big Don was at the stables grooming one of his thoroughbreds when he heard Fritzi barking. He handed the reins to the stableboy and went to have a look. He saw Luke's car parked in the drive on the other side of the gates. The boy himself was leaning against the gate with a large sports bag slung across his shoulders. He looked tired. Fritzi stood nearby, snarling in a friendlier way now he recognised the interloper.

"You've got balls lad coming here," Don said, "I have to give you that." He hesitated and nodded at the bag. "What have you got there?" he asked.

"Can I show you?" said Luke.

"Yes, but carefully now. Slow and steady."

Luke unslung the sports bag, rested in on the gate and opened it, then pulled out the bronze cauldron he'd taken from the house.

Don's eyes widened. "Is that what I think it is?" he asked.

"Yes, it is," said Luke.

Don eyed the cauldron covetously. "You better come inside then," he said. He watched as Luke weakly tried to push open the gate. "You're hurt," he observed with some satisfaction.

Luke looked down at his side which was bleeding again. "It keeps reopening," he said.

"Fair enough, for what you did to my boys."

"They're not *your* boys though, are they?"

Don shrugged. "All the same, don't expect Maude to be pleased to see you."

Luke hesitated. "Why did they do this?" he asked. "Gordon and Gideon, to their own children."

There was a silence while Don chewed the matter over. "They have different priorities to us," he said eventually, "that's the best way I can explain it. Something to do with having a foot in both camps. The one as can do that has Time as their playground. That's what they say."

"I see," said Luke. He wasn't sure he did. All the same he followed Don painfully towards the farmhouse next to the stable.

"Do you think this makes up for what you did?" asked Maude.

"I don't know," said Luke. He was very weak now and the room kept swimming around when he tried to look at it. The three of them were at the kitchen table, with the cauldron at the centre of it.

"He was set up by all accounts," said Don. "We all were."

"I see, and you reckon I should release you from your oath, do you?"

"Well, that's up to you my love of course."

"Not so easy to do. Let's see." She picked up the cauldron and turned it over to look at the base. There was some writing embossed upon it. "Property of Medea," she read. "This is the one alright. Hmm." She seemed lost in thought for a while. Everybody waited. "Go outside and get a fire going," she said to Don after a few minutes, "Let's see if this thing works."

Once the fire had got started and the cauldron filled with water and suspended over it, Don went to the freezer and took out the dismembered portions of my body that they'd kept stored in there. There were two arms, a torso and two legs. Maude seemed especially interested in the torso though.

"Look," she said, "its swollen."

Luke and Don looked: the frozen chunk of meat was indeed distended around the stomach.

"Pregnant?" Don asked.

"Sort of," she said. "More like its hosting something."

Luke kept himself propped against one wall. Maude had treated the wound and given him some sort of mineral shake to drink and he felt a bit stronger. All the same he couldn't be sure that everything he was seeing or hearing wasn't the result of a discombobulated brain. He watched as they took the body parts outside and added them to the cooking pot. It was early evening now, just starting to get dark. He could hear the pot simmering as they returned.

"Did you bring the mixing stick," Maude asked him.

He looked up, trying to focus on her words. He was a bit slow. "Er no, I left it behind," he said at last.

She looked him up and down, at the wound in his side especially. "Yes, I see," she said. "Well, now things make more sense. Never mind, I think Don has an old chopper he's not using, I'll make the best of that." Then she found the wood axe and took it outside and stirred the pot, threw in some herbs and did a bit of chanting. There was nothing really to do then but wait. Luke tried his best to stay awake but grew faint and eventually sat down and laid his head on the kitchen table and passed out.

When he came round it was dawn and light was coming in through the window. He blinked his eyes and looked up groggily. Maude and Don were by the door open to the outside, listening to a mewling cry coming from the direction of the pot. Everybody went out. It was crisp and fresh, the morning light making the dew in the fields glint. They went over to the cauldron, where the fire was just embers, and looking inside, saw that the water had simmered away and a new babe was nestling in the bones at the bottom of the womblike vessel, making shrill desperate cries. Maude reached inside and picked him up, rocking him gently until his crying began to subside. She inspected his arms and legs, fingers and toes and genitals. Everything seemed to be present. She cooed and chucked him under the chin and then peered more closely.

"Ooh look," she said, "he's got gills."

Luke made the drive back up to the tree where my head was buried. The crows were following him now. He could see a flock of them overhead, above the overdue car as it drove along the motorway. Once he got there, he sat down next to the hawthorn.

"So, how did it go?" I asked.

"Good," he said. "They told me where the house was anyway. It's just a bit more of a drive."

"Think you'll make it?"

"I'm not sure." And the crows were getting confident now. Some of them had come down to land on the car, as well as the nearby wires.

"That would be a shame. I'm thinking your mother would be in her mid thirties by now. About the right age, you could have a proper relationship."

"That would be good. I'd like that." He looked down. His side was bleeding again. He closed his eyes and swayed a bit. I was worried if he drifted off, he wouldn't come round again.

"Hey Luke!" I shouted.

"What?" he mumbled.

"Time to get going."

"Not yet," he said, "just a little rest." He laid down on the grass. It felt cool and good.

I waited a little. "Luke?" I said. There was no answer. All I could hear was the cawing of the carrion.

The Geas

"So how are you related to the deceased?" the police officer asked.

"I'm his godfather," Gideon replied. Yellow police tape had been fastened around the tree and then around the car to form a cordon. Luke had been put in a bodybag and taken away.

"What about his actual parents?"

"His father disappeared some time ago and his mother is in Wales. I'll have to call her. The boy had something of a troubled childhood I'm afraid."

"He has a sheet. Any idea who could have done this?"

"None whatsoever officer." He looked at the tree with its scarlet flowers. Just then a starling descended to perch on one of its branches, carefully avoiding the thorns.

"Gideon and Gordon buried my head here," it chirped. Gideon was shocked of course, but kept his composure. The police officer looked around to see who had spoken, looked at the bird, then looked at Gideon.

"Did you hear something?" he asked.

"No officer, why?" said Gideon. He looked with relief as the bird flew off.

The policeman looked puzzled then shook his head. He'd been covering shifts and was probably tired. "It doesn't matter," he said. "If we have any more questions, we'll be in touch. And we'll need an address for the mother.."

"Yes, of course," said Gideon. "I trust you'll let me break the news to her first."

"Ah well," said Rhiannon, "perhaps its for the best. And I have little baby Dylan to comfort me again." She looked down at the wee babe. He gurgled and wiggled his fingers and toes and blinked with one set of eyelids. They were all sat in the garden of the Welsh cottage - her, Gideon, Maude and Don - even though it was a slightly cool and damp Spring day. Still there was blossom on the tree and daffodils coming up through the borders.

"Fiona is making over the cottage to Gordon and Blodwyn," said Gideon, "so I'm afraid you're going to have to go back to Paul's old place."

"Will we?" Rhiannon thought about this. "Well, maybe that won't be so bad. I mean, I know Paul always worried about the first Dylan fitting in, but I think people are a lot more tolerant nowadays."

"Have you spoken to Paul lately?"

"No." She pondered this. "No, I haven't. Perhaps I'll stop for a chat when we go past."

"It might be a good idea. Perhaps you could ask him to stop spreading gossip about us, while you're at it?"

"Gossip. What sort of gossip?"

As if to illustrate the point, a lark came down and landed on the apple tree and started to sing:

"Gordon and Gideon buried the head

Of a man who wasn't dead

And a tale he had to tell

To the worms and birds as well

Of men who kept on swapping places

So you could not trust their faces

If one is here and one is there

Who is the girl with scarlet hair?"

Rhiannon sighed. "Well, yes," she said. "Paul did always have trouble letting things go."

They all met at the border by the hawthorn - Gideon, Rhiannon and Dylan in the 4 by 4, and Gordon and Blodwyn in a moving van. They got out of their vehicles and faced each other, like a set of almost perfect mirror images, except Gordon had the missing eye and Blodwyn wore a floral dress while Rhiannon dressed in delicate pastels. And then there was Dylan of course. Gordon was talking to me via the tree.

"You need to stop it, Paul. Tell the birds to stop spreading their malarkey."

"Or what?"

"Or we'll dig you up."

"Oh, I'm not so sure about that Gordon. I'm entwined among the roots of this tree you see. Even got one growing through my eye socket. It would mean cutting down the tree, excavating the roots, all on the site of a recent crime scene. Hard to do without making people suspicious, don't you think?"

"You always were an irritating twat, Paul."

"What are you going to do about it though?"

"Why don't you tell me. What will it take to shut you up?"

"Oooh, let me see. I was thinking .. one gets the chance to do a lot of thinking down here you see, not much else to do as a matter of fact .. I was thinking .."

"Yes yes! Get on with it you annoying spunkweasel."

"How about if you were to plant another tree in the garden?"

"That's it. Plant a tree?"

"One with golden apples."

"You mean like golden delicious?"

"No, I mean like golden apples. Apples. Made of gold."

"Oh .. I just knew you were going to be a tosser about this. Where am I meant to find something like that?"

"The Hebrides."

"Yeah? How do you know?"

"Bloke down the Stag told me."

"A bloke down the pub told you there was a golden apple tree growing on an island out next to the ocean somewhere. You know why they call them the Outer Hebrides, Paul? Because they're out in the middle of fucking nowhere. And the island, I don't suppose he mentioned which one?"

"Fraid not."

"No. And there's nothing more to this? You just happened to be discussing metallic fruit."

"He told me a story, about a man who was on holiday in the Hebrides, and his landlady gave him a golden apple, and when he got back home he gave it to his wife instead of his mistress, and .. well, let's just say it caused a lot of conflict."

"Right, and this landlady ... "

"Runs a B and B called the Nine Witches, on the Isle of Lewis."

"So, I just go up there, ask her about an apple, and then there's no more tittle tattle."

"That's all there is to it."

"Right .. right." Gordon turned and went back to the party and walked up to Blodwyn. "We're off to the Hebrides," he said.

"We are?" she said, looking disconcerted, "What for?"

"Because .... that Paul is being a typical fucking titbrain."

"Why can't we just go to the cottage?"

"Because the birds will be spreading gossip about us, to everyone in the village."

"Does that matter?"

"Does it matter!!! That we're ...."

"We're what?"

"We're ..."

"That I'm a prostitute and you're a schizophrenic. Why can't you just say it?"

"Well yes, it matters actually. Tell them Gideon."

Gideon was looking on awkwardly. "He's right. It wouldn't go down well. I can imagine them getting up some sort of petition against you."

"So that's it you see, we're off to the Hebrides."

"No, you're off to the Hebrides."

"Oh, it's like that is it?"

"Yes, it is."

"And what are you going to do, go back to being a fucking trollop?"

"I'll look after the cottage. The birds only gossip when you're around anyway."

"I see," he said, bristling with anger. "Well, just try and keep your fucking legs closed while I'm away, will you?"

"Sure, and why don't you try not to be completely fucking deluded?" The situation was getting a bit tense.

"Everything will be fine," said Gideon, trying to calm the matter down. "Let's not get into a disagreement at this stage, not now everything's almost settled."

"He's right," said Gordon, pacing up and down to work off some of his irritation. "It's just this one last thing. I'll drop you off and take the van up to Scotland." And with all that decided, everybody crossed the border, with Rhiannon and Gideon going east, and Gordon and Blodwyn driving west. It looked like some strange kind of conjunction.

 The Nine Witches was a converted crofter's cottage near the coast. From the beach nearby you could see Great Bernara, then some of the smaller islands and beyond them the Atlantic. Not too far away was a prehistoric stone circle. Gordon parked up the moving van outside and looked around. There was a brisk wind and some gulls had settled on the sparse grass nearby.

"Headburier," one of them cawed.

It was irritating. The problem with the birds was they were everywhere. He masked his fury and went over to the cottage and rang the bell. It was an old type, where you pulled the chain and the clapper struck against the dome, making a clanging chime. Eventually a lady answered the door.

"Hello," she said, in a pleasant Scottish brogue. "You're not here about a room, are you?" She looked at the van. Maybe it was a delivery.

"No," said Gordon. "I'm here to ask about a golden apple." He figured he might as well get straight to the point.

"Oh, it's that is it. Well, you better come in then."

She opened the door and led him into a small dining room that had been turned into a sort of reception area. "Can I get you a cup of tea," she asked. "Maybe a scone?"

"Sure," said Gordon. "A scone would be nice."

He sat down on a floral upholstered armchair and looked around at the white plaster walls. There was a driftwood coffee table and an old dresser and opposite him a large mirror. He looked at himself with his one eye. The mirror seemed to exaggerate the scar, twisting that side of the face. He looked away quickly.

The landlady came in carrying a tray with a pot of tea on it, and a plate of scones and two small dishes with butter and jam.

"I see you were looking at my mirror: mirror on the wall," she said.

"Yes," he mumbled as she put down the tray and turned to look at it herself. He glanced up at it quickly, and saw that in her reflection she was older and snakes writhed in her hair. He looked away again.

"I know," she said. "It tends not to flatter. My sister has a much better one."

He cut a scone in half and spread it with butter, then ladled on jam with a small spoon.

"You must get a lot of tourists stopping here," he said, "with the stones nearby."

"I get my fair share," she said, sitting down. "Not many return visitors though. I can get you a brochure, if you're interested in the stones."

He munched his scone and shook his head. "Not really why I'm here," he said.

"The legends say they were giants, and turned to stone for being heathens. What do you make of that?"

"It's a good story. I heard a different one though, about an apple."

"Single minded sort of chap, aren't you?"

"When I have to be."

"Well, there is an apple tree that's true. Not on this island though."

"Which one, then?"

"You know, I was thinking about that mirror. My sisters is really a lot nicer."

He sighed and spoke sardonically. "You want me to go and get it for you I suppose?"

She perked up, as though the idea had just occurred to her. "Oh, could you?" she shrilled. "That would be splendid, and I'd be grateful of course."

He nodded ruefully. "And your sister, where does she live?"

"A bit north from here, on the Faroe Islands."

He calculated, then spluttered his tea a bit. "The Faroe Islands? Thats nearly fucking Iceland!! Pardon my French."

"It is dearie, but there's a chap I know runs sightseeing trips out there. You might even get to see a dolphin. It's true, the waters will probably be a bit choppy ..." She paused thinking about it. "A couple of months time would probably be better."

"No, fuck that. We're doing it, we're doing it now."

"I'll go have a word then, see if I can get him to take you out."

"Fine." She got up and looked at him. He seemed tense. "Don't worry about it," she said. "I think you'll find you and my sister have things in common."

"You doing alright there, lad?" asked the skipper concerned. The rough Atlantic was bouncing the motor boat up and down on its turbulent waves, and occasionally from side to side too. Gordon gripped the side of the boat looking soaked, pale and miserable in a borrowed macintosh. Another blast of salt water came overboard and flung itself in his face.

"Aye," the man continued. "Not the kind of voyage I'd recommend for a landlubber, not in these conditions. Cheer up though, you might see a dolphin." Gordon looked out at the ocean, he couldn't see anything but a tangle of wind and water and foam. The light though, he noticed, was getting thinner as they moved further north. It had a spectral twilight quality. "Won't be getting proper dark out here for a long while," said the skipper. "Not even at night. You'll see the sun and the moon and the planets too. Ain't no surprise really, people used to think this was the edge of the world. Hyperborea, that's what they used to call it."

When they got to the island, the skipper took a while to land, avoiding the sand banks. It was a small, rocky isle lashed by wind, with puffins clinging to the crags. Gordon got off the boat, his yellow coat slick with briny water.

"People live here?" he asked.

"Not for thousands of years is what they say, not until the Scandinavians turned up. That's what they say mind," replied the skipper.

"The woman I'm looking for ... "

"Mad as fucking box of frogs.. she lives on a croft right on the westernmost tip, overlooking the ocean.

The island being so small, directions weren't hard to follow, nor did it take long to find the house. Sheep were grazing on the tough clumps of grass nearby and the ocean was loud, you could hear it battering the cliffs. The house clung to the rock like a low stubborn beetle. He went through the gate, walking past a neatly stacked pile of logs and knocked on the front door with the heavy brass door knocker that was nailed to it. The lady took a long time to answer it. When she did, he saw that she was incredibly withered and old. She was hunched over and her skin was like brittle yellow paper and only thin strands of hair remained attached to her bald head. She was gummy, with only two remaining crooked teeth, and seemed almost blind, with one rheumy cataritic eye and one empty socket. It didn't seem feasible to Gordon that she could survive out here, never mind prosper. She tightened the woollen shawl she was wearing and grinned at him like an imbecile.

"Yesssss?" she tittered. She had a strong Scandinavian stopglot accent.

He tried to grin back. "Hello," he said, in an overloud voice, in case the old bat was deaf as well. "I've come from your sister, over on Lewis."

She nodded. Her hearing seemed okay. "My sister, is it? And how is she?"

"She's okay, she thought you might be interested in selling your mirror."

"My mirror?" She tittered again, "so she thinks I'll be losing my marbles does she, that I be giving such a thing away?"

He shook his head. "Not give it away, sell it. I can do you a very good deal."

"Can you now?" She stared at him unseeing, although he still had the unnerving sensation of being observed somehow. "Why don't you come in and tell matters for yourself then?" She went back into the house, leaving open the door and he followed. They passed through a stone flagged kitchen, with rudimentary cupboards and a stone worktop. A hearth had been made in the centre below the chimney and an iron pot was suspended above it. The living room was very small, with rugs over the wooden floor, an iron fireplace containing ash and a half burned log, and two armchairs. The mirror, unlike her sisters, was freestanding and occupied a corner next to a table with a radio. The old woman went and stood in front of it.

"Come and be looking then," she said "and tell me what you see." He stood behind her and looked into the glass. In the mirror she was young and pretty, with long curling blonde hair, a fine figure and two bright eyes that looked back at him.

"Ah," said the crone, "now I see you. A callous face and you have the eye missing like mine. There's a solution to that though. Go into the bathroom and get my glass eye, it's through the door just there. I want to look at myself again, just once more"

Look at *herself*? Still, he went through the indicated doorway into a narrow white tiled bathroom, quite clean, and looked around until he noticed the cupboard over the sink and opened it. Inside, next to a packet of medicines and a jar of salve, were two glasses, one containing dentures and the other a glass eye suspended in antibacterial fluid. He took it through and watched as she hunched over further and inserted it with a plunk, looking at, into the mirror this time. It seemed like she could look *through* the eye.

She giggled with delight. "Ooooohh yes," she said. "Aren't I pretty? Aren't I a dish? So lovely, don't you think?" She turned to face him. The eye was horrendous somehow, livid and glaring, it stood out from her face like a patch of liverwort on a rockface.

"A beauty in your day, " he replied.

"In my day," she laughed. "But awful now, is it? So tell me, for what price would I part with such a mirror? It's not just myself I am seeing here either. I see lots of things. Past and future. I know what is bringing you here for a start."

"Then you know," he said, "that I won't be leaving without it." He looked around, there was a metal poker hanging next to the fireplace. That would do.

When he left the building, he had the mirror under one arm and a brand new eye. He'd looked at himself before leaving of course. He'd looked strong, younger and more vital than ever, back to his old self. He'd found a wheelbarrow outside, taken the old lady's body to the cliff and dumped it over the side. Be a while before anyone looked for her, he reckoned. Only the sheep seemed judgemental. They watched him as he walked away from the house, back towards the boat. Even though it was day, the moon was overhead, with its one eyed face and the sun nearby.

 "You got it then," said the landlady of the Nine Witches, as she watched him remove the mirror from the back of the van. "Got yourself a new eye into the bargain," she observed. He was parked outside the bed and breakfast. There was one other vehicle there, a green Yamaha motorbike. Apparently, it belonged to a guest.

"I struck a good deal," he said.

"You must have," she replied, appraising him. "Well, it's done. Bring the mirror inside and I'll meet my part of the bargain. You can take the old one if you want .. it's something of an antique .. "

They took the old mirror down from the dining room wall and propped the new one up in the corner and she wasted no time in setting herself before it, observing the new reflection with obvious satisfaction. She looked fresh and regal and her hair was now only tumbling chestnut curls.

"Much better," she said. "Yes, I'm pleased."

"So, I get the apple?" asked Gordon.

"I'll take you to the island tomorrow, yes. In the meantime, I suppose, you can spend the night here. I'll turn down one of the rooms."

"Okay," said Gordon. It was a shame about the guest he thought. After catching a glimpse of her in the mirror, she'd begun to look rather fetching. But it would be good to sleep also. It had been a long trip.

 Something woke him up during the night, the sound of an engine. He got out of bed in his underwear and went to the window. The motorcycle was turning onto the road leading away from the hostelry, its headlight beaming out into the darkness illuminating some conifers. He tried to make out the rider but he was just a dark huddled mass. Engine roaring, the bike headed off in the direction of the standing stones. He waited until the whine had faded away and the lights of the bike were no longer visible then went back to bed.

The bike was absent when they left the house the next morning to make their way down to the shore, but Melinda, as she'd decided to be called, told him no matter: the guest had decided to make an excursion, that was all.

"In the middle of the night?" asked Gordon.

"Sure, why not?"

"Inconvenient, isn't it?"

"Not really. In all probability, they'll be back before they set off."

"Right." One of those quaint highland phrases, Gordon decided. They found the skipper berthed not too far from one of the hotels near the bay. They'd got there early, so as to get to him before the tourists. He'd been setting up a sign advertising whale watching trips. Gordon watched as Melinda talked to him. Occasionally they turned to look in his direction. He had his new eye back in, and apart from it twitching of its own accord now and again, he found it fairly comfortable. She beckoned him over and they were on their way.

The boat went down the strait past Bernara and then out into the sea. They made their way around several small islets and then over to one craggy outcrop that seemed uninhabited. There was only one place to put ashore, a narrow stretch of rocky beach, but the skipper took the boat past that round to the cliffs on the far side.

"No one lives here?" asked Gordon.

"There's some herders rent land, bring their flocks across in the Summer," said Melinda, "but it's owned by a rich banker in London. He comes over about twice a year to conduct ceremonies. Right now, it should be empty."

The skipper brought the boat to a halt. It rocked about on the tide, swaying one way then the next. The cliffs reached up above them to their left, a few rocks sticking out of the waters before them. Gordon looked up. He could see the wiry apple tree that had rooted itself into a crevice on the side of the rockface. Something glinted among its small tough leaves. Gulls circled overhead.

"That's it is it?" he said. Melinda nodded. "One apple every ten years or so, if you're lucky."

The skipper was getting some ropes and crampons from the back of the boat. It was almost as though he'd known their destination all along.

By the time he got back, Blodwyn was waiting for him at the front of the cottage.

"That didn't take long," she said, as he was getting out of the van. "Almost as if you were no time at all."

"It felt like a bloody long time," he said, "believe you me."

"But you got it?" Strangely, she didn't seem to notice the new eye, as though he'd had a pair of them all the while.

He got the golden crab apple out of the glove compartment and held it up. It shone bright and lustrous in the sun.

"My hero," she said.

He grinned wolfishly and gave her a kiss and a quick slap on the behind. "Oh, and I got you a present too," he said.

"A present. What kind of present?"

"A mirror: mirror for the wall. Tell you what. You get that apple planted and I'll get it out of the van."

He threw her the fruit and while she was taking it out back, he retrieved the mirror and took it into the house, propping it up on the mantelpiece. He must have been tired from the journey because he found the mirror really difficult to lift, the weight almost causing him to hunch over and his steps were small and faltering. After lifting up the mirror, he paused to gasp for breath. He stepped back and had a look and then stared appalled at his reflection. He was a wizened old man, with a liver spotted head, bald except for three greasy wisps of hair. He was gummy and toothless and drooled down his chin. Worst of all was his eye. While the other was yellow and saw through a blur, as though the world were smeared, the glass one faced off to the side and twitched, making him seem demented. In fact, when it looked back towards him, it seemed to be actively mocking him. He heard the back door open. Quickly he grabbed a brass figurine off the mantelpiece and hurled it at the mirror shattering the glass, then he leaned in and tipped it so that it fell on the floor.

Blodwyn rushed in. "What happened?" she exclaimed.

"I was clumsy, it fell off," said Gordon.

"Aww, that's a shame."

"Never mind. I'll buy us lots of nicer things. Now we have the house and the money." He grinned at her.

"I'll get the dustpan and brush," said Blodwyn.

While she cleared up the mess, Gordon went out and looked at the garden. There were rosy red apples on the tree and early autumn flowers in the border, even as some of the leaves on the plants yellowed. A small circle of upturned soil in the middle of the lawn where the turf had been dug up and the golden fruit planted. A magpie landed in the tree. It looked at him for a while, then flew away, without saying a thing.

The Quest

"What happened?" asked Gideon. The funeral was over, and while Fiona was weeping and Rhiannon was attempting to console her, over by the wall of the village church, he had taken Blodwyn off to one side, to try and garner some details

"I don't want to talk about it," she said.

"The coroner said the cadaver was atrophied, as though it had been dead many years. He can't account for it."

"All I know is .. we were celebrating his return, with a spot of bedroom gymnastics, when he had a heart attack and keeled over, and then he just started .. turning into a husk.. Oh no, I can't .. ugh.." She started shaking. It was hard to distinguish between her being upset and traumatised. "**All that was left was a glass eye,**" she wailed, becoming hysterical, "**and it was looking at me!**"

"There, there," said Gideon, attempting to put a comforting arm on her shoulder, as the vicar and some of the villagers looked over.

"Oh Gideon!" She threw herself into his arms.

"Look on the bright side," he said. "You can grow out your hair now, you can be yourself. Maybe we can get something going?"

She looked at him through tear stained eyes, first at him then round the cemetery. "This isn't really the time or place," she said.

"But you'll think about it?"

"I suppose so."

"Good, that's all I'm asking." They separated and altered their demeanour to something more appropriate as Rhiannon and Fiona came over, Rhiannon pushing Dylan in his pram. He was munching on a shrew.

"OOh look at him," cooed Blodwyn, peering into the pram, "they grow so fast nowadays, don't they?"

"I know," said Rhiannon. "I've only just bought the pushchair and he's learning to walk. Another year and I'll have to try and get him into preschool, although how we square that with the council, I've no idea. I have enough trouble with him not having a proper birth certificate. Paul says skip school altogether: by the time he's old enough for infants he'll have finished puberty anyway."

"And then what?"

"A curse on the child I say," said Fiona.

"Come on now mother," said Gideon, "it's time to let all that go."

"No, a curse," said Fiona, "once I've had time to think of something. What I can't believe is you're still talking to Paul."

"Well, he is the child's birth parent. Father and mother now, really. Besides, I find it relaxing," said Rhiannon, "being a tree has made him a lot more philosophical."

That was true I suppose, and as Dylan grew up, he started to make regular visits which I looked forward to. Gideon and Blodwyn had got married and once a year, Rhiannon would take him over there for a visit and they'd stop at the border. The strange thing was, Dylan confessed to me when he was four, that the pair of them never seemed to grow any older, even while other people in the village aged and even passed away. Also, they'd never had any children so there was no one down there to play with, which was a shame, because the pair of apple trees in the garden had grown ancient and dropped fruit so all around the cottage now was a wonderful orchard of red and gold apples. Sometimes, they used to add the fruit to the stews they were always making in Fiona's old cooking pot, that Maude had given them as a wedding present: apparently bearing her former lover little ill will. It was this that had provided Fiona the inspiration for her curse. This had happened just before she went away, taking nothing with her but Gordon's glass eye and broken mirror as mementos, and it has to be said, by now she was getting fairly senile. The curse had seemed pretty harmless, that Dylan might never marry until he inherited the cooking pot, and under normal circumstances would not have presented a problem, except for the couple's peculiar refusal to age.

"Now the problem is, the house has moved again and we can't find it," he was saying. He'd come on his own this time, in the car he'd just bought. A tidy little Fiat, although he'd had to have the roof removed, what with him growing so fast: he was nearly eight foot tall already and not even through puberty! An awkward stage, and I got the impression he was rather self-conscious about his gills and webbing. Hard enough to meet girls without a curse being laid on you!

"I'd go and look for it myself but mum won't let me on my own. She says I'm growing up too fast for her anyway. I go over there for a week and I'd be seven when I got back: not even a young man any more, never mind an adolescent."

"She wants to hang on to you, you can't blame her."

"But I'm going to need to find the pot eventually, if I want to get married."

"True also, that mixing rod's not much good on its own. Maybe you could get folk to find it for you?"

"Like who?"

"Got any mates?"

"Not many. I don't really fit in is the problem, except when I go to Aunt Maude's. The people down there are more accepting somehow."

"Auntie Maude! There you go. I bet she knows someone could be persuaded to go find Gideon. Why don't you pop down and see her?"

"I could do that, yes. I have a friend down there, Kay, he was on about forming some sort of club. Like a charity, we fix people's problems in return for fealty, or something of that nature."

"There you go, that's the way to go."

"Thanks pops! You always give good advice, and your blossoms are looking good this year! Still scarlet, maybe getting a bit pinkish."

"Yes, that reminds me. There's a place you want to look out for, hotel called the Red Lodge. You find that, I bet your uncle's place is nearby." He patted the tree, then got back in his car and drove back to my old house to pack some stuff.

It was when he was halfway down to Aunt Maude's that the next incident occurred. He was crossing the iron bridge that spanned the river when he saw that his path was blocked by a sports car that had broken down, apparently skidding so that it obstructed both lanes. He brought the Fiat to a halt and got out. The bonnet of the sports car was up and a young man was looking at the engine.

"Problem?" asked Dylan.

The man looked up and smiled apologetically. "Yes, I'm afraid so," he said with a French accent. "Smoke started coming out of the bonnet and then the engine cut out."

Dylan went over to have a look. "It's flooded," he said. "We need to drain it. I've got some hosing in the back of my car."

"Thank you," said the man. "My name is Lance by the way."

"I'm Dylan." They shook hands. "Let me get the hose. I reckon we can fix this before any more traffic comes along." They spent the next twenty minutes draining the sump, with the river flowing underneath them, making rippling noises. "There you go," he said when they were finished, "try that."

Lance got in the car and turned the key. The engine spluttered then caught, revving up noisily. He beamed.

"I'm so very grateful," he said. "Which way are you going?"

"Down to the low country."

"So am I! Maybe we can travel down together."

"Sightseeing are you?"

"Something like that yes. There's a hotel down there I'm meant to be staying at."

"Which hotel?"

"The Red Lodge, do you know it?"

"No, but I've heard of it." Dylan hesitated. "Our meeting you know, maybe it wasn't a coincidence."

"Oh, you don't think so?" said Lance, looking out from his car with a twinkle in his eye."

"No, I'm thinking not."

"Who knows, mes amis." He revved his engine again. "Shall we go?"

Dylan smiled and nodded, picked up the piping and oil canister they'd been using and returned to the Fiat. He started it up, honked his horn to say that he was ready and they set off together.

 "So," said Lance, "ou est le mysterious femme?" They had been at Maude and Don's for about a month having various adventures, and Lance had been learning to ride at the stables. In the meanwhile, Maude had been mulling over the matter of Dylan's curse. I suppose in some way she still felt motherly towards him, having been his midwife, so with that in mind, one afternoon she took him down to the fens. It was a cool autumn day and down by one of the lakes, where a wooden pier had been built among the reedbeds, a mist had gathered. They went to the edge of the pier and waited, while the mists over the water thickened, obscuring the horizon.

"Dangerous out there now," said Maude. "If we're lucky a boat will pull in." Eventually it did, a narrow houseboat painted a gay yellow with jolly floral patterns stencilled across the prow. It came out of the vapours first as a vague shadow, and Maude turned on the torch she'd brought, guiding it towards the pier. Then you could see the colours and a woman came out of the cabin. She picked up a mooring rope and tossed it towards Dylan, who quickly caught it and tied it to one of the posts supporting the walkway. Then they pulled the boat into harbour. It was only then that Dylan looked at the woman properly. She was fair, tall, with lovely variegated gills and a dorsal fin atop her brow. He was smitten straight away.

"So, she is tres jolie, this lady of the lake?" asked Lance.

"A rare one," said Dylan, "and with me being owner of the mixing rod, she has agreed to an engagement."

"But not le marriage?"

"Not without the cauldron."

"Ah, sacre bleu!"

"A pity I know, for from what she says, she has much fine spawn waiting for me in the lake."

"I will get the cauldron for you!"

"It is too much to ask ... "

"Nonsense, and the members of our club, all those who swore fealty, they must search too."

"I suppose .... "

"Of course! Much prestige it brings them, membership of the Round Table, and a good percentage of all our illustrious doings. Now is the time to prove their worthiness, and in truth, there is nothing un bonne homme prefers than to prove his worthiness before les autres, even if he does not really understand what for."

So that night they met in the clubhouse, and there was much quaffing of lager, and an excitable Lance got everyone to commit to finding the pot, swearing an oath upon Dylan's mighty mixing rod, which they all agreed should be called Excelsior.

The next day he set off for the Red Lodge, which had just recently re-appeared in the area, on an industrial estate next to the recycling centre. Luckily, his booking was still on the system and he was able to get a room. He was awoken during the night by the sound of a purring engine. He got out of bed in his boxer shorts and went to the window and looked out. There was a Yamaha motorcycle outside in the car park, which was otherwise empty apart for his own vehicle parked further to the right. The motorbike was underneath a lamp post, which shone its beam down on the rider, who wore a thick dun green parka jacket with the hood pulled up tight so you couldn't see his face. No crash helmet. Lance had the intense impression the rider was waiting for him, that he should go down, get in his own car and follow him, but for some reason he was afraid. The man waited a while as they stared up and down at each other, Lance silhouetted in the window, then revved up the engine and rode away with a screech.

The next day he woke up. His memory of the man on the motorbike was vague like a dream. Maybe that was what it had been. He dressed and showered then went back down into the lobby and looked out. The car park was full, just as it had been when he arrived. It was a dream. He found his car and drove off in what he supposed was the direction of the house.

Lance was one of the last members of the club to return almost six months later. Not one of them had come close to finding the house, never mind got as far as making an offer for the pot, and many of them came back older. This was especially true for Lance, who claimed to have got lost and was now middle aged. He lamented much over his wasted youth and spoke of highways that led to nowhere and roundabouts that took him back where he started and long periods of time where he'd had to abandon the search and take on menial jobs so he could afford to continue, or at least find his way back to the low country, for wherever he went the communication networks seemed to be down. There had been affairs and temptations on the way of course but then always the fear of being lost forever and the need to continue.

"So how did you get back?" asked Dylan. They were sat together on the pier by the fens with their feet in the water. Dylan had come several times, especially on misty days to see if he could lure the boat back to shore but so far with no success, which he was finding frustrating.

"It happened as I was leaving a petrol station and approaching a junction," said Lance, looking out across the reeds to where a flock of geese were making an occasional dive into the waters. "The motorbike was ahead of me, it waited until I was close and then made a tournez le droit and this time I followed it. The road brought me back to the Lodge and here I was after all that time." He spat bitterly.

"I couldn't have known it would be so difficult. I'm sorry actually Lance."

"It doesn't matter." Lance kept on looking out over the lake.

"You're just saying that aren't you?"

"Oui, seeing as you asked."

"Well .. maybe I'll leave you for a bit. If there was anything I could do to reverse the situation I would of course."

Lance didn't say anything else, so he left him looking at the lake. At some point the mists drifted in and then Lance was gone.

 After that there was only one lad willing to have a last shot at breaking the curse. To be fair though, he was new to the group and maybe not in full possession of the facts, and also a bit naive - simple minded according to Kay, who had only let him join because he might be daft enough to actually go looking for the house, now that everyone knew the dangers.

Gavin he was called and he had little problem finding the Lodge, although he had to get there by bus. His possessions he was carrying in a plastic carrier bag. He booked a room and asked the receptionist for a map of the area and then went to his room to start planning what route he was going to take from here.

That night of course he was woken by the sound of an engine. He got out of bed in his pyjamas and went to the window. The motorbike with its beparkaed rider was outside, revving the engine of the Yamaha. The rest of the car park was mysteriously void of vehicles. Gavin wondered what the man wanted. He thought he better go and find out. From the window he signalled the rider that he would be five minutes, then got dressed, gathered his belongings and went outside. He crossed the blank tarmac over to where the hooded man was sat waiting, small clouds of exhaust gathering in a skein around his wheels.

"Everything alright?" he asked.

The rider nodded an affirmative, then motioned that Gavin should get on the back of the bike. Gavin hesitated, then shrugged and got on the back, carrying his plastic bag. The driver revved the bike and sped out of the car park, leaving the glass fronted building behind. They headed down the road until they reached a junction. To the left Gavin could see the lights of a petrol station. The rider ignored this and went straight on. Half an hour later they were at the edge of a great orchard and the man brought the bike to a halt and let Gavin dismount. Gavin looked at the man and tried staring into his hood, but it was too dark. There was nothing in there but shadows.

"Why have we stopped here then?" Gavin asked.

The man pointed at the wood. Gavin looked at it.

"Seriously?" he said. "I don't think so mate."

The man shrugged and powered up the bike and before Gavin could do anything it had sped off again, kicking up a shower of dirt.

"Oi!" shouted Gavin. "Oi! That's not funny tosser." It was still dark. The road seemed to go a long way in each direction. He turned to look at the wood and his foot kicked something. He stooped to pick it up. It was a golden crab apple. He looked again at the trees. Dylan had said something about an orchard now that he thought about it. He put the apple in his bag and sat down waiting for the morning.

Gideon was tasting the stew when he heard a knock at the door. He frowned. It had been a long time since they'd had visitors. Ones who knocked anyway. The village had pretty much forgotten they were here, now that they were cut off by the forest and most of the people they'd met when they arrived had grown old and passed on.

He went into the front room and listened. The knock came again. "Blodwyn" he called. She came downstairs, the red hair flowing to her shoulders. "Did you hear that?" he asked.

"No, what was it?"

"A knock." It came again, a third time. She jumped slightly

"That's peculiar," she said, "Maybe we should answer it though. It could be a child from the village, got lost while scrumping apples."

That brightened him up. "Do you think so?" he asked.

She nodded eagerly, so he went into the hall and opened the front door. Gavin was standing there. His clothes were torn and face scratched, as though he had gone through thorn bushes. He still had the carrier bag though and a rough beard to boot.

"Hi there," he said, smiling amicably. "I'm a friend of Dylans. We've been trying to find you."

"Friend of Dylans is it?" said Gideon, slightly put out.

Gavin nodded.

Gideon sighed. "Then I suppose you better come in," he said. "I must say, it looks as though you've been in the wars."

"Yes," said Gavin, as they entered the front room. "That orchard of yours, its bigger than it looks. Snakes in there too, great big ones."

"Ah yes, them. Didn't give you too much trouble, I hope? They do keep the rodents away from the crops."

"Well, they were a bit lively .. " He nodded politely at Blodwyn. "Mainly it was the time it took to get here. Get the feeling I've been wandering around for weeks."

"You must be hungry then, why don't you sit down?"

Gavin did so, feeling awkward as Blodwyn just stood there and smiled at him.

Gideon came back in carrying the cooking pot. It was fresh off the stove and steam was coming out of it. "Would you care for some stew Gavin?" asked Gideon, placing the pot down on a mat on the coffee table.

Gavin had a look. Something about the stew was a bit unappetising, even though the journey had left him truly famished. He thought it might be the fingers floating in it.

He smiled weakly. "Not sure I'm ready for stew to be honest," he said. "Maybe something a bit lighter." It's not what the pot serves, it's who it serves, he thought to himself.

"Lighter, oh dear." Gideon and Blodwyn looked at each other. "I'm not sure we have anything lighter," he said, "do we dear?"

"No," she said. "We tend to stick to the stews."

"Ah, never mind," said Gavin. "I'll just wait till I get back."

"Are you sure?" said Gideon. "You must be really hungry."

"No, I had a lot of apples, probably made me a bit bloated."

"You're sure?"

"I'm sure, but it is the pot I needed to talk to you about."

"I'll make you a cup of tea," said Blodwyn. Gavin nodded relieved. Gideon was putting the lid back on the cauldron. "How do you mean?" he asked.

Gavin wondered where to start. "It's about this curse your mum put on Dylan, we're trying to get it lifted."

Gideon frowned. "Really?" he said, settling himself down in the opposite armchair.

"I'm afraid so."

Blodwyn brought in the tea. She tilted her head slightly, as though listening for something upstairs.

"I'll be back in a moment," she said. "I just need to check on something in the spare room."

Gavin left the house carrying the pot. He was about to go back into the wood, when Blodwyn opened the front door, looked over her shoulder, then scurried out holding something wrapped up in a blanket.

"Quick, take this," she said in a hushed voice. She very quickly put the object in the cauldron. "He won't miss one, not if I'm careful."

Gavin looked over towards the door, nodded without saying anything and set off back towards the Lodge.

And so, you will be relieved to hear, the wedding took place and what a splendid occasion it was, by all accounts. Rhiannon was there, resplendent in white and almost outshining the bride Neve, who came to shore aboard her gaily painted boat, now festooned with flowers, as was the pavilion on the adjacent bank. Dylan turned up in Lance's old sports car and then the ceremony took place in a nearby chapel, and afterwards there was wine and dancing, with members of the Round Table all attempting to outdo each other with their leaps and acrobatics, as they tried to impress the ladies that Neve had brought with her as bridesmaids, and these too pranced merrily around the great maypole that had been set up, making a display of their fins and flippers.

Also in the sports car was Gavin as best man, who to everyone's surprise, after setting off for the Lodge had returned with the pot after a couple of days, although his bedraggled appearance suggested that the affair had taken much longer and proved more arduous than seemed feasible over such a short period of time. Certainly, he had grown in wisdom and character and was accompanied by a mysterious child to boot. This he introduced to Rhiannon as her nephew, explaining that her sister in law wished to have it fostered, their own locale becoming increasingly isolated and offering little in the way of opportunity for their offspring. Indeed, it was noted how well Gavin and Rhiannon were getting on together. Everything was finally coming around full circle.

"I'm sorry you couldn't attend," Rhiannon was saying to me. Spring was underway and I was in full bloom, my boughs garlanded with fresh pinkish white flowers. "I think you would have enjoyed it."

"So, Dylan is all settled down now is he?" I asked.

"Oh yes, they're spawning already, lots of little critters, although it's hard to get them out of the water. They love to swim."

"It's good that they're active. Maybe they could come and see me sometime." I liked the idea of having grandkids.

"I think that they'd like that," she said, "especially now that you're a relic." It was true, the tree was now a gnarled old specimen. "They're going to be passing this way quite often anyway, delivering the agreed sacrifices to my brother. They might even stop and perform one or two here."

"I don't know, if that's the kind of thing I really want to be associated with."

"That's up to you of course. I will say, we're raising up little baby David specially. He'd look pretty good nailed to your branches, that's the thing."

"I just can't get used to all these new customs. They seem a bit grotesque." Maybe though, I was just out of touch.

"You don't mind though, me and Gavin?" she said.

I didn't mind very much. Mainly what I wanted to do was sleep. It seemed to me, down in the sod, it was hard to keep track of what was real anyway. Maybe I was getting things mixed together. Maybe I was imagining things.

Maybe, just maybe, I just made the whole thing up.